Mrs. Watson has been an educator for over fifty years, having a B.A. in History and Religion, as well as an M.A. in Secondary Education and School Administration. Her thesis on 'Writing About Novels of the Revolutionary Era' gave her an added specialty in History. She continues to teach English and History to high school students and loves the dynamics of the classroom. She enjoys reading, doing jigsaw puzzles, scrapbooking, and, of course, writing, in her spare time.

Dedicated to Steve, Steven, Sharron, Scott, Mariann, and Hal. Thank you all for your encouragement during the writing process.

Special thanks to my Lord and Savior, Jesus Christ.

Shirley Watson

THOMAS SINCLAIR MEETS THE SWAMP FOX

The American Revolution in South Carolina

AUSTIN MACAULEY PUBLISHERS™

LONDON * CAMBRIDGE * NEW YORK * SHARJAH

Ordering Information
Quantity sales: Special discounts are available on quantity purchases by corporations, associations, and others. For details, contact the publisher at the address below.

Publisher's Cataloging-in-Publication data
Watson, Shirley
Thomas Sinclair Meets the Swamp Fox

ISBN 9798891550988 (Paperback)
ISBN 9798891550995 (ePub e-book)

Library of Congress Control Number: 2024901488

www.austinmacauley.com/us

First Published 2024
Austin Macauley Publishers LLC
40 Wall Street, 33rd Floor, Suite 3302
New York, NY 10005
USA

mail-usa@austinmacauley.com
+1 (646) 5125767

Sharron Bounds, for buying a book on the Swamp Fox to assist in my research.

Steve Watson for research on some of the battles in South Carolina during the Revolutionary War.

Chapter 1

It was the end of November 1780, in the midst of the American Revolution for Independence, and young Thomas Sinclair stood listening to the sounds of the night all around him. He could hear the horses nickering in their enclosures. Somewhere nearby, soldiers could be heard whistling and humming tunes that were unfamiliar to the fifteen-year-old lad, whose life was normally tied up working with horses on his father's farm in New England. But, because his older brother, Benjamin, had joined the Continental Army and was fighting elsewhere, Thomas had to stay home to help his father on the farm.

As much as he loved working with the horses, Thomas would rather have been with his brother, fighting as a loyal Patriot for independence and freedom from Britain.

However, one day, as luck would have it, Thomas was given a rare opportunity to display his courage in another way. Just recently, his father had reluctantly allowed him to help deliver six thoroughbred horses to his close friend, General Nathanael Greene, who now headed the Southern Department of the Continental Army.

So, now, here he was, standing outside General Greene's tent, listening to the private conversation going on inside. He didn't consider it eavesdropping, just putting his ear to the ground so that he could tell his father some interesting things happening here in the Carolina war zone. As he stood listening to the general, another name came up—Francis Marion. Thomas had heard of this man before but had neither seen nor met him.

He knew about his reputation and the fact that many people called him the Robin Hood of this time in history. Now, getting his mind back on the discussion, he heard more exciting conversations come up. Had he actually overheard what the general just said? Now, what was it he said again? Did he say that he needed someone to deliver a message to Colonel Marion?

That would really be adventurous, thought Thomas. *I know I could do that if only given the chance. Nah, they wouldn't let me do it. They would say I was too young!* then he reckoned, *If I don't ask, how will I ever get to be involved in this war?* Without thinking further, in case he should dismiss his own idea,

Thomas knocked on the tent flap. All conversation inside came to a halt. General Greene's aide, George Singleton, asked, "Who is there?"

"It's just Thomas, Sir. May I enter, General Greene?"

"Of course, Thomas," answered the general. "Are you getting packed up to head home with the two men who came with you? Is there anything you need before you go?"

Thomas sighed. It was now or never!

Then he said, "I wasn't being nosy, General Greene, Sir, but I heard you mention the fact that you needed someone to deliver a message to Colonel Marion. I...I...I was wondering if I could be of service to you," he stuttered. "I have completed the task my father assigned me, that of bringing your horses to you, so I am free to assist you in any other way that I can."

"Hmmm! What about your father, young Thomas? Won't he be wondering why you are taking so long to get back home? I would not wish to send you on a possibly dangerous mission without your father's agreement, nor would I want to risk the relationship your father and I have because of his disapproval."

"I don't think that will be an issue, Sir, especially if he knows I am running an errand for you," Thomas ventured. "I know that I can do this!"

"I have no question about your ability, Thomas. After all, you did stealthily bring six beautiful horses to me for my officers. My main concern is that the part of South Carolina that you would be headed to is now under British control, for the most part. Tell me again, why you think you can deliver this dispatch to Colonel Marion."

"Well, Sir, to be honest, it may be a little intimidating but I have already traveled many, many miles skirting around British sentries and camps to get this far with a string of horses. Going a little farther into hostile territory won't be a problem for me, especially since I will be traveling alone." Thomas stood facing Nathanael Greene with almost a pleading look in his eyes, but he would not beg for this opportunity. He silently awaited the general's decision.

After much stroking of his chin whiskers and rubbing of the back of his neck, the general capitulated. "All right, Thomas. The job is yours. What I will do, however, is send a letter back home to your father, explaining the reason for your absence from the farm. I will let him know that you volunteered, as there was no other person available to deliver my message to Colonel Marion. Hopefully, your father has enough men on the farm to assist him while you are away."

"Now, go and prepare your gear, get your horse taken care of, and enjoy a good night's rest. It might be the last good rest you will have for a number of days. I want to see you back here by 6 o'clock tomorrow morning."

"Yes, Sir!" Thomas responded as he quickly headed out to do what the general had commanded. He had already eaten, so that wasn't a problem. He just needed to go to the cook and get some foodstuffs to take with him on this journey. Not knowing how long the trip would take, and not knowing the unforeseen incidents that might arise, Thomas wasn't quite sure of how much to take with him. While his stallion, Ebony, was 16 hands high, he did not want to burden his horse with unnecessary items.

He did need his rucksack and a blanket or two because it was late November and winter was nearly upon them. Even in the South, it was starting to get rather cool in the evenings, even downright cold, at times. After gathering everything he could possibly need, Thomas headed to his bed in a nearby tent.

Visions of danger, wild animals, and British Redcoats filled his dreams, causing him to spend a restless night with very little sleep. All too soon, light began filtering through the tent flap, and Thomas was awakened by footsteps and voices outside his sleeping quarters.

A soldier called out, "Are you in there, sonny boy? The general is ready to give you your marching orders."

Thomas answered groggily, "I'm awake. Give me a minute. I'll be right there."

"You'd better hurry, is all I'm saying. Our general does not like to be kept waiting!" With that, the soldier stalked off to report that Thomas was on his way.

Within two minutes, a record for Thomas, he was standing in front of General Greene receiving the dispatch meant for Colonel Marion. "Be quick as you can, lad. This missive is important to the war effort. Go speedily but be cautious and be very careful when speaking to strangers. Your very life may depend upon it! On your way, then, and God speed."

Chapter 2

That send-off by General Greene had been five days ago. His foodstuffs were practically all gone; he hadn't delivered his missive, and had seen neither hide nor hair of the elusive Colonel Marion.

Now, here he was, a loyal Patriot of the Revolutionary cause, sitting astride his own black thoroughbred, Ebony, and having absolutely no idea where to go or even where he was. Thomas scanned the countryside looking for any sign of Colonel Francis Marion and his band of men. Still nothing and no one to be seen!

He had been on the road long enough, he thought, and was more than ready to reach his destination, carry out his errand, and return home. The last he had heard of the colonel's whereabouts was that he was camped and headquartered in the swamps surrounding Snow Island which was located in the lowlands of South Carolina. He had been told by various people he had met on the way that Colonel Marion would appear quickly, attack the unsuspecting Redcoats, and then disappear into the swamp.

He learned that these surprise attacks on the soldiers were called guerilla warfare tactics, a new idea to Thomas. These stealthy maneuvers were used to continue to keep this area of South Carolina out of the hands of the British. Marion's reputation seemed to be well-deserved from what Thomas had heard about the man. It appeared that Marion's cunning, resourcefulness, and determination helped keep the cause of American independence alive here in the South.

After seeing nothing promising in the distance, Thomas shifted in the saddle, rubbed Ebony's glossy mane, and muttered to himself, "Where can that man be hiding?" Ebony snorted as if in answer and Thomas smiled at the four-legged friend that he had raised from a foal. Ebony's withers rippled under Thomas's hand, as if in acknowledgment that they might actually be lost.

Never having been this far South, this was new country to him. Even the smell in the air was not the same as in his home state of New Hampshire. Some of the animals and vegetation that he noticed were not familiar to him, and somewhere, nearby, there was supposed to be an island in a swampy area. The question again was, where? In which direction should he go?

While ruminating on those questions, he noticed a cloud of dust about a half mile away from his position. *Oh, good!* he thought. *Maybe some answers to my questions are coming toward me.* Suddenly realizing that he was a stranger to the Carolinas, and knowing that British troops were trolling in the area, he decided that the best thing for him to do at this point was to hide and be an onlooker for a while, at least, until he could determine why men were riding their horses so rapidly toward him. Spying a small grove of trees close to the road, he directed Ebony to that spot to await the newcomers.

Thomas crooned softly to Ebony to keep the nervous horse quiet. Was it danger or relief that was speeding toward them? As the cloud of dust rolled onward, Thomas strained to see who might be approaching. Flashes of red and green came into view, and Thomas was glad that he had hidden in this small copse of crape myrtle trees. A unit of British cavalry was almost upon him.

Now what should he do? Play ignorant if discovered hiding in the trees? Couldn't very well show innocence if he's found hiding, could he? Should he pull out his musket? What a dilemma!

His thoughts were answered as the group stopped right in front of his hiding place. Staying concealed was the best alternative! He only hoped that Ebony would not nicker when he heard the other horses. He didn't have to worry, however, as Thomas had trained Ebony well, and he stood silently awaiting his master's command.

Thomas's tension almost caused him to have heart failure. When the men began to complain to their commander, he listened closely. One of the Greencoats was truly frustrated, and he exclaimed, "We've lost him, again, Sir! IIc just seems to vanish into thin air! How can we catch him, when we can't even see him? His men appear, strike us swiftly when we are least expecting it, and then disappear just as quickly back into the swamp! There just seems to be no way to catch him, especially when he seemingly melts into the atmosphere and becomes a part of it. It's like he's a ghost!"

Colonel Tarleton, the commander of this cavalry, was beside himself. He had to agree with his sergeant that Marion and his bushwhackers lurked in the murky swampland, waited for the British to get close, struck them savagely, and then hightailed it back into a swamp that left no tracks for the Green or Redcoats to follow. Here they were, near the end of 1780, and he was still no further ahead than when he was assigned this region to take out the wily Francis Marion and his brigade of country hicks.

After all, Marion's band was made up of only untrained men having to scavenge for food and ammunition, weren't they? "Lord Cornwallis has no idea what he has commanded me to do," muttered Tarleton.

"Sergeant, I know exactly how you feel! While we were back there sloshing around in the muck and water, Marion was probably sitting back on his horse and having a great laugh. I can hardly wait to get my hands on him! I have had enough of this running around for nothing today, so let's head back to camp. Anyone would have trouble finding and catching this Swamp Fox!" So, wheeling his horse around, Tarleton galloped away as he led his soldiers in the opposite direction from which they had come.

Thomas muttered to himself, "Well, that was certainly interesting! He actually called him a Swamp Fox. That's a really good name for someone who uses the swamp as his home base. I have done my share of fox hunting at home, so I know how cunning they can be." He laughed out loud, glad to see that the British had been outdone, again, and he had witnessed their annoyance about being outwitted and foiled one more time.

He's certainly a sly one, that Swamp Fox, Thomas thought. *On top of that, I know that General Greene considers him to be a very able military leader. His plans are ingenious and he carries them out methodically.* He had also heard that Colonel Marion had his men put white feathers in their hats so that they would recognize their own men and not shoot each other in battle. "Now if I could find Marion, I would put a white feather in my hat, as well," he surmised.

But, the white feather would have to wait until he found Marion and delivered his message from General Greene. He still had a mission to complete.

"Okay, Ebony, where do we go from here? We can't go in the direction of the British, because we would surely be caught and General Greene's message would fall into enemy hands." Ebony snorted in reply. "That means we had better head in the opposite direction. Hopefully, we will be able to find Marion's headquarters."

By now, it was starting to get dark, and if he couldn't find Marion soon, this would be another night sleeping all alone under the stars. Thomas wasn't anxious to do that, so he hustled Ebony down the road, hoping against hope that he would run into Marion's men, sooner rather than later. He needed to pass on the letter and let Marion know what the British colonel had said about him. Maybe, he would get a good laugh out of that.

Coming upon a narrow path farther down the road, Thomas muttered to Ebony. "Well, boy. This trail doesn't look too well-traveled. Let's try this one and hope that the swamp isn't too far away."

For the next hour, Thomas pushed through thick underbrush and short, scrubby palms, not seeing the resemblance of anything that could be used for a hideout or headquarters. Where was Colonel Marion located, anyway? By this time, even though it was almost dusk, he and Ebony were sweating profusely from the humidity, and Thomas was completely done with the buzzing gnats and flies surrounding him. He couldn't go on much longer.

Both he and Ebony needed rest, and he was feeling rather hungry. His poor horse probably was, too. "We'll just roam a little further down this dusty footpath and then we'll stop, my friend."

As Thomas wound his way down the trail, his thoughts were centered on the man he was going to see: Francis Marion, the colonel. He was the only senior Continental Army officer left in this part of the South. He had heard of Francis Marion, even had read an article about him in the news bulletins at home. He had heard that he was quite the roughneck, owned his own plantation, and would not live under British rule.

He also had heard that Marion was an expert at guerrilla tactics, whatever they were. He supposedly had learned about fighting this way while serving during the French and Indian War against bands of Cherokee. Thomas loved the fact that Colonel Marion would attack the British dragoons and Loyalists by night, and then retreat into the swamps, of which he had a thorough knowledge, to sleep by day. On top of that, he had several encampments set up and would and could change camps at a moment's notice.

He would also post sentries at all times. Those guards would warn him and their allies of approaching danger from the enemy. Another thing that set Colonel Marion apart was his love of horses and his superior horsemanship. In Thomas's eyes, Marion was a true Patriot, and a hero.

Knowing that Colonel Marion was probably the most wanted man in the South, Thomas was anxious to deliver his dispatch to him. Since they were hunting him in every swamp, he was afraid that the British would find the warrior before he did. Now, if he could only find his way to the correct hideout.

Chapter 3

Rounding a bend of the trail in the sand hill region along the Pee Dee River, Thomas suddenly came upon two men engaged in a conversation. "Good grief, they are standing right in the middle of the path!" He grumbled. There was no way to get around them on horseback, so he cleared his throat loudly to get their attention. Finally, they noticed him there and backed away to allow him to pass.

As Ebony got abreast of the men, one hollered out, "Hey, do you know where you're going?"

Being a truthful and polite young man, Thomas answered, "I really don't know, Sir. I may even be lost." Not sure what these men might be up to, Thomas didn't want to give away the fact that he was looking for Colonel Marion. They could be Tories, for all he knew, and the Tories sided with the British in this war. As General Greene had pointed out, one had to be extremely careful when speaking to strangers.

"Well, youngster, if you continue in the direction you're going, you'll be in alligator territory," said the other man. Being called a youngster rankled Thomas, as that was a term he had to put up with at home, but he shivered at the statement, nonetheless. He understood that the involuntary shudder up and down his spine was not from the cold weather! He knew enough about the South to know that he didn't want to encounter any of those dangerous swamp creatures.

The men appeared to be sizing him up, as if not quite sure of him either. Maybe they were considering the fact that he may be a Tory spy. Thomas had to think of something fast! What should he do or say? As he stared back at the men, he noticed that they were wearing white feathers in their hats. Why hadn't he noticed that before?

Debating whether to tell them who he was, Thomas considered the consequences if he gave the wrong information. Would he be captured and imprisoned or welcomed into the fold, so to speak? The only way to find out would be just to blatantly state that he was looking for Colonel Francis Marion, so he said, "I have heard that men who follow Francis Marion wear white feathers in their hats, and I notice that both your caps have white feathers. Are you gentlemen a part of his brigade?"

Jonas, the younger of the two men and the one who had spoken first to Thomas, asked him, "Who are you, that you would want to get that kind of information from us, especially since we are strangers to you? We see no need to answer any of your questions! We don't know you!" With that said, he pulled his pistol and pointed it at Thomas. "Climb down off that horse, right now!" He commanded.

"What kind of madness is this?" Thomas huffed. "Is this how all newcomers are greeted in the South?"

"Yes," said Jonas's friend, Luke. "Especially when we don't know that newcomer. So, as my companion ordered, get off the horse!"

Not sure what to do but comply, Thomas slowly stepped down, keeping Ebony's reins in his hands.

Luke snatched the reins from Thomas and began guiding them further into the swampy area that almost surrounded them. Thomas had not observed earlier how close he had actually ridden to the swamp. As they advanced into the boggy area, Thomas was immediately overwhelmed by the foul odor that engulfed the three men.

"Eew! What is that stench?" He questioned. "What a stink!"

"Oh, that's rotting vegetation mainly," said Jonas. "That's what gives it that rotten egg smell. Added to that are the odors from the alligators, fish, and of course, just the muddy water in the swamp. Take your pick. You get used to it after a while."

Thomas didn't think he could ever get used to that odor, and he needed desperately to hold his nose. Since they had already called him a youngster, he wasn't going to act like a weakling, so he suffered the smell. His most urgent thought, right now, though, was where this walk might take him. He sincerely hoped that it would be toward the man he needed to see.

"How much farther?" He asked. "It seems as if we've been traipsing through the muck for hours. Where are we going, exactly?" Obviously, they hadn't been following a straight path but one that wound its way around every tree and plant. Thomas realized that these men were just trying to confuse him so that he wouldn't be able to find his way back to wherever they were heading.

"We'll be there, shortly," Jonas replied. "Just be patient. We know where we're going."

Not long after this exchange, a voice rang out. "Halt! Who goes there? If you belong here, give the password. Otherwise, turn around and go another way! This is private land."

Thomas looked at his two companions and wondered what was going on. Finally, Luke puckered up his lips and let loose with a whip-poor-will song.

"What on earth?" Thomas mumbled. He recognized the call of the whip-poor-will because he had heard it multiple times at home, especially in the evening. As he waited to see what would happen next, Luke melded his whip-poor-will song into the haunting call of a loon.

Hmm! What's all this about? he thought.

Immediately upon hearing the correct countersign, Eli, the sentry, gave his okay for them to continue their trek into the marshland. Unbeknownst to Thomas, there had been more than one person guarding the little trail upon which they were traveling, and after a few more paces, the glint of firearms along the trail alerted him that they, indeed, were not alone! Thomas could only surmise that they were nearing their destination, whatever and wherever that was.

In the growing darkness, it was hard for Thomas to see the features of the men, and as he stumbled along, not unmindful of the men hustling him, his mind kept soaring to places he didn't want to see, namely his upcoming future. How terrifying it is when you are so unsure of what life holds for you around the next bend. This was exactly the predicament in which he found himself. Right now, he couldn't picture his imminent future, so how could he view himself as a soldier for his country?

Struggling with these thoughts, he determined that whatever was ahead of him would have to be dealt with, somehow, so he started to take stock of his immediate surroundings. *Okay, what's around me?* He started to take inventory: black gum trees, swampy muck, the stumps of mossy cypress trees, alligators, brush, narrow paths, snakes, and everything else he couldn't see. Wow! Not much help there, but maybe, thick enough to hide in, if he could escape his captors. But how would he escape? He didn't even know, yet, what they would be doing with him.

He continued thinking. What would be the best way to evade them, if indeed he could escape? Was there anyone who might help him to get free? Could he get to his pistol hidden in his saddle bag? And what about Ebony? He couldn't leave his equine friend behind! While he was pondering all of the decisions he might have to make, Luke and Jonas came to a full stop. Ahead of them was an encampment of some kind.

Thomas's fears came to the forefront as he thought, *This is it! What's going to happen now?* All of his calculations about escaping immediately flew out of his head. Oh, he was so frustrated with all of the hassle: the reins of his horse taken out of his control, being jabbed in the back with a pistol, walking through the stench of a swamp, and not being told a solitary thing! *Come on guys, give me a break here!*

No help seemed to be coming from any quarter, especially when Jonas, who had his pistol still pointed at him, nudged him in the back with it. It seemed that he really meant business! "Go on, kid," he said. "Keep ahead of me and slowly walk toward the camp." Thomas had no choice but to do what was ordered. His questionable future loomed ahead of him.

Chapter 4

As they neared the campsite, Thomas noticed that they had, at some time, crossed onto a solid island that was on a rise overlooking the water. He wondered if this was actually Snow Island! Now, walking farther onto the isle, he could see some small boats and canoes tied up along the shoreline. He could hear the low melodious speech of the South and soft laughter from several men who were standing or sitting around a large fire. He could also smell food cooking, and his mouth started to water as he realized that he hadn't eaten since this morning's scanty breakfast of dried bread and cheese.

Could his long journey finally be at an end? Would he meet Colonel Marion here, or someone else? What if this wasn't supposed to be his destination? If it were, what if they didn't believe what he had to say? Oh, well, he did have the dispatch from General Greene. Surely, they would know then, that he was a Patriot! Oh, wait! What if these men weren't Marion's?

His mind was put at ease, however, when Luke yelled out, "Colonel Marion, Sir! We have a guest!"

All heads turned toward Thomas, who now felt like a little bug under a magnifying glass. One of those heads had a little leather helmet on it, and below that were steely coal-black eyes which seemed to look straight through Thomas. The man, himself, was not very big and possessed the body of a gangly teenager, even though Thomas knew that he was about forty-eight years old. He was dressed in a crimson vest, of a coarse texture, and his leather form-fitting cap, which covered his receding hairline, was inscribed with the words, 'Liberty or Death'.

Nervous tension ran up and down Thomas's backbone. This had to be Colonel Francis Marion, the South Carolinian roughneck for whom he had been so diligently searching.

"Well, now, who do we have here? What has brought you to Snow Island? How did you get here? Are you friend or foe?" Those questions and more came at Thomas in a fast clip, and Thomas was stymied. By the way he was being questioned, there was no doubt but that this was Marion, the leader of this band of men, and the one to whom Thomas was to deliver Greene's missive.

Thomas stuttered out a quick answer. "M…m…my name is T… T… Thomas Sinclair, S…S…Sir, and I was sent by Ge…Ge…General Greene to give you an important message from him." Getting over his fear and stuttering, Thomas said, "It has taken me several days to find you, Sir, and I hope that the information is still relative. By your leave, Colonel, I will retrieve the packet for you."

Colonel Marion gave his nod of approval and Thomas slowly walked to Ebony and withdrew the letter from his saddlebag. Handing it to Colonel Marion, he commented, "I assume that I am handing this over to the right person."

Chuckling, Colonel Marion said, "You have found the right person, son." As he walked away, glancing at the letter, he called out, "Simon, take care of this young man's horse. He is a beauty, so take good care of him. He's probably ready for a good drink of water and food as well." Knowing how much Colonel Marion admired beautiful horses, Thomas was not surprised that the colonel would take Ebony into consideration at the outset.

"Yes, Sir," Simon responded as he took hold of Ebony's reins and led him to the small pasture that housed several other horses.

"Come along with me, young Thomas," said the colonel. "We will sit over here by the fire, where it is brighter. You can tell me about your trip and what you have observed along the way."

Thomas had noticed earlier that Marion walked with a pronounced limp and wondered what had happened to cause that. He wanted to ask about it but feared it would be rude to ask. Marion had seen Thomas watching his gait and beat him to the punch. "I see you looking at the way I walk. Unfortunately, from birth I have had bad ankles and knobby knee joints, so that's a part of my unusual hobble. The other reason is actually a longer story," he said.

"During March of this year, I was at a friend's home for a dinner party in downtown Charleston, just before the British laid siege, and eventually took the city in May. The toasts went on and on, and I was starting to feel hemmed in by all the noise and rowdiness. I am not a drinking man, but I had been enjoying myself, maybe a little too much," he said with a grin. "So I decided that the best thing to do was to leave the party, but as usual, our host had locked all the doors in the house to keep his guests from leaving before the fun was over."

"So, what did you do, then?" Thomas asked.

"I have no idea what I was thinking! Maybe that's the problem, Thomas. I definitely was not thinking straight! Anyway, I decided to just jump out of a window. That was a regrettable decision on my part because the window was on the second floor and a little too high for my five-foot-two frame. My recklessness was rewarded with a broken ankle!"

"Knowing that the British would be looking for me, I had to hide away with friends and relatives until this corrupt ankle had healed enough to support my weight. Alas, it has left me with this pitiful limp. If it weren't for my faithful servant, Buddy, I wouldn't even be walking this well. He has nursed me through the whole thing. The Lord bless him!"

"I know that must have been painful, Sir," Thomas stated. "I broke my arm once, and I can commiserate with the frustration that you have been feeling. Colonel Marion, before you read your letter, may I mention something that I overheard on my way here?"

"Surely, Thomas. What is it?"

"Well, Sir," Thomas said. "Just a few hours before I came across your men, I was almost waylaid by a small British cavalry. They happened to stop right in front of my hiding place and they were complaining about not being able to find you. The interesting part was that their colonel referred to you as a 'Swamp Fox'! I thought that was quite an extraordinary term, since you are headquartered here in the swamp and you are as cunning as a fox!"

Marion lifted his head and laughed heartily. "Did you hear that, men? The British are calling me a Swamp Fox. Maybe we can continue to outfox the enemy with our foxiness!" Leaving his men in laughter, he continued sniggering himself as he continued on to the firepit.

"Well, young Sir, let's see what kind of message you have brought me from the good general." Marion withdrew the letter from its pouch and began to read.

While the colonel was scanning the dispatch, Thomas took the opportunity to study the man in front of him. The leader of this ragtag bunch of volunteers was not really handsome with his long thin face and hook nose. Thomas thought that the man probably would not have been found too attractive by the ladies. But, his flinty demeanor and confidence in himself would push all other thoughts of his outward appearance from anyone's mind.

The manner in which he conducted himself would have readily garnered respect from his soldiers, as well as his superiors. Thomas surmised that this was not a man who would suffer disrespect to himself or to his small brigade, so he determined to stay on the right side of this colonel.

Taking the time to look at his surroundings, Thomas counted about twenty or so volunteers, some black, some white, and a few Indians. Simon was still tending to Ebony and the other horses. The two men who had brought him into camp, Jonas and Luke (also known as Lucas), were eating and drinking, while some were just sitting around their own little fires talking and laughing softly. Even though they all seemed to be doing their own thing, Thomas got the impression that as soon as the colonel spoke, they would be on their feet, ready to do his bidding.

As he considered everything and everyone in the camp, Thomas suddenly heard his name, not loud, but low and distinct. He turned his head to find that Colonel Marion was speaking to him.

"Thank you for delivering this message in good time, Thomas. General Greene has asked for our help in an important plan to outwit the enemy. The engagement with the British will be soon and we need to be ready to assist. You have arrived soon enough with this request and we can now move forward with the general's command. We need to get the men together to discuss it, but before we do, we need to see to your comfort, as much as possible in this swamp, as it's been a long day for you, already. You haven't eaten yet, have you?"

"No, Sir," Thomas replied. "Something sure smells really mouth-watering and I could use a good meal right about now!"

"What we have to offer is scant but there's a tasty sweet potato dinner cooking over the fire. There is plenty to share, so help yourself. Sit down anywhere, and after you have eaten, we will all take a look at General Greene's letter."

Thomas said, "Thank you, Colonel," and moved over to where the food was located. He found a pewter plate and cup and served himself a healthy helping of the meal. Finding a seat on a log close to the fire, Thomas wolfed down his meal, using his cornbread to sop up the gravy. He had been hungrier than he thought, and though he was not overly partial to sweet potatoes (a staple not common in the North), the food was soon finished. Wiping his mouth on the sleeve of his shirt, he looked expectantly at Colonel Marion who had seated himself on the other side of the fire.

The colonel was deep in thought, and Thomas sensed that he was wrestling with an idea of how to complete the orders that the general had sent him. Looking up suddenly, he peered at Thomas.

"Thomas," he said, "do you know the contents of this letter? Did the general mention anything of significance about this message? I know you're young but have you had any fighting experience, yet? What will you do now that you have completed your mission? As our ranks are low right now with many men away taking care of their families, would you be willing or be able to assist us in carrying out the general's request?"

Thomas gulped. The questions had been fired at him in true Francis Marion fashion. He didn't know how to answer and wasn't sure where to begin. The logical place would be to begin with the first question, so he answered, "No, Sir. I do not know what the letter says or what it concerns. I just know that General Greene wanted you to have it as soon as possible."

Thomas continued in this line of answering, telling the colonel that his father had sent him to deliver a string of horses to the general, who being a good friend of his father, had asked for six horses to be delivered to his officers. Thomas went on, "I had brought the stallions from our horse farm in the Northeast down to the general's camp. I had already dropped off the horses, and then learned that General Greene needed someone to deliver a message to you, so I volunteered."

"I had heard much about you, Colonel, and felt it an honor to be able to meet you. As far as fighting goes, the only shooting I have done is at ducks or deer. But, I am a loyal Patriot, and am willing to serve my country wherever I am able. So, if you need me, I am at your service." That had been a long speech for Thomas, and he wiped the sweat from his forehead as Colonel Marion kept staring at him.

"Well said, Thomas. I think you are a very courageous young man. If you are willing to join the other men assembled here, you would be a welcome addition to my little band." Chuckling to himself, Colonel Marion continued, "However, after we discuss what must be accomplished, you may change your mind and head back to the farm, lickety-split. Now come and meet some of the officers and men that you will be standing beside in battle."

Without further ado, the colonel walked to the edge of the clearing and called out in a clear voice, "Gather around, men. I want to introduce you to our newest member. Lads, this is Thomas Sinclair, late of New England, and just arrived. He has a dispatch from General Greene, which we will be discussing momentarily." Glancing at Thomas, the colonel said, "Look around at this group of men, Thomas, and get to know them. They may be called upon to save your life sometime in the future."

Leaving Thomas's side for a minute, the colonel motioned to two men who had been standing together observing Thomas.

"Come over here, fellows, and let me introduce you. Thomas, these two are Hugh and Peter Horry. They are brothers, as well as successful rice and indigo planters. They are not only close friends of mine but two of my most trusted confidantes. Peter, here, commands our mounted brigade, while Hugh commands the infantry."

Pointing to another of his men, he said, "This is Major John James, who is an excellent advisor to me. He has other family members within this group, as well, one being his son, William, who is of the same age as you, Thomas, fifteen, I believe. Is that correct, John?" Major James nodded his head in affirmation.

Marion continued speaking. "You will get to meet the rest eventually. We are all just a mixture of Patriots, Thomas. You will find planters, poor farmers, family members, Irishmen, Presbyterians, Huguenots, Scotch-Irish, teenagers, Africans, and many Indians in our band, as well as others, like yourself, Thomas, who are willing to help us fight. We are all activated by the love of country. But, above all that, Thomas, we are all friends who have one singular aim, to rid this country of the Redcoats."

"Now, friends, on to the important business of young Thomas's errand. First, you all know that General Greene is no supporter of our militia but he knows that in order to finish this war successfully, we must act cooperatively."

Before Marion could go on, Hugh Horry complained, "Why doesn't he get help from Washington, Sir? Our numbers are so thin that we barely have enough men to go around!"

"In answer to your question, Hugh, General Greene cannot get any help from the North as far as reinforcements go. General Washington needs all of the forces in the area to keep an eye on the British soldiers stationed in New York. The British will never willingly give up South Carolina because of its position on the Atlantic Ocean. They need those piers and harbors for their ships to bring needed supplies and troops. So, in order for the Patriots to retake

South Carolina, he will have to rely on us. We are all there is in this part of the country."

"Sir, General Greene doesn't even like us! We are considered far below his idea of what fighting men should look like, and how they should be trained. He says that all we can do is pillage and plunder, and that is so far from the truth…!" Peter Horry groused.

"That is all true, Peter, but the general has capitulated on that and has commended us for our services in this region, that is, being able to keep the British soldiers from extending their claim on all of South Carolina. He wants us to continue appealing to the people, namely the Tories, get in their good graces as much as possible, and bring them to our side. But, that is not what he is asking us to do right now. His immediate request is for us to acquire information regarding the enemy's plans."

"You mean become spies, Colonel?" Thomas asked. He wasn't sure that he was cut out to be a spy. He knew what had happened to Nathan Hale, who was an American Patriot, soldier, and spy. He had volunteered for an intelligence-gathering mission, but was captured by the British and executed by hanging. Nathan Hale had only been twenty-one years old, and Thomas was only fifteen, yet.

"Yes, Thomas, that's exactly what he means. Come on, men. Let's put our heads together and come up with a plan. We may not like this assignment because it is dangerous, but as General Greene stated in his letter, 'Spies are the eyes of the army'. He really needs this intelligence! He said that it is of the highest importance that he get the earliest information on any British reinforcements arriving in Charleston."

Chapter 5

"What do you mean you lost him again? General Cornwallis stormed."

"I am sorry, General, but the man is a veritable ghost when he gets close to the swamps," Colonel Tarleton complained. "We chased him for seven hours, over 26 miles, through all kinds of brush and swamps. He just kept out of the range of our sharpshooters. We just couldn't keep up with him. He had a head start on us and he knows those swamps like the back of his hand. We were unable to catch him. He is just like a sly, old fox, Sir. I truly regret that I was unable to catch him, General, but I have not given up yet!"

"I have got to get Marion out of that part of South Carolina. He must be caught! We know that he is low on ammunition and has to forage for food. How his men can remain with such a renegade, I don't know!" Cornwallis exclaimed.

"Well, Sir, you will be glad to know that even though I didn't catch Marion, I was able to burn down many houses and plantation homes of the rebels in Marion's part of the country. I left women and children sitting in the cold beside their burning homes with nothing to protect them, except for what they were wearing. I didn't spare Whigs or Tories, just in case some of those Tories had turned to Marion's side."

Tarleton sounded very proud of his cruelty to the families of the rebels. What he seemed to lack in ability, he made up for in his incredulous lack of compassion. He was definitely out for the win, and the temporary feeling of triumph made him boastful and blustering to the general. Although Cornwallis said nothing of Tarleton's behavior, he felt that even if Marion had been disconcerted with Tarleton's actions, Marion would be out scouting for those ruthless Redcoats as soon as he was able.

With Tarleton's brutal tactics, Cornwallis knew very well that they were not done with Colonel Francis Marion, not by a long shot!

Continuing, he berated Tarleton by saying, "Marion has been having success after success, and we have got to subdue him, and get him out of the way of our soldiers. Otherwise, we will not be able to hold South Carolina for much longer! Do you understand that, Tarleton?"

"Yes, General, I completely understand the necessity of that, but he has patrols spread out everywhere in the countryside. It's impossible to contain him or his band of men."

"I don't care how impossible it is, Colonel! Just get it done, and done soon! If that man isn't caught, we will be going home in disgrace! He will be the ruin of His Majesty's army! Any blow to us cuts deeply. Our reinforcements are not getting here as fast as we need them to, and I am anxious to have fresh manpower because I am preparing to invade North Carolina again. Even with Marion still running around loose, South Carolina seems to have quieted down somewhat, and I can continue North. But I do need those new recruits that have just landed in Charleston."

Cornwallis continued, "If Marion finds out that I have new reinforcements on the way, he will surely stop them somehow. We must protect those untried recruits on their journey here. Since I don't have any extra regulars to send down to Charleston to help bring them here, we'll have to march them through territory not controlled by Marion. He is too threatening, and those raw recruits will be sent running hither and thither if they come across that fearsome old fox."

"So, here's the plan: We will march the troops Northward from Charleston to a plantation not located on the Santee River, which is where Marion is apt to be. Then, after they reach the plantation owned by Sumter, we will have an infantry of fusiliers guide them farther North until a cavalry unit from Camden meets them and leads them the rest of the way. What do you think?"

"Sounds like a perfect remedy to that problem, Sir," Tarleton stated. "Now if we can just keep Marion from hearing about the plan and the reinforcements, it will go without a hitch."

"That's where you come in, Colonel. You must find him and keep an eye on his activities every minute that you can. I suggest that you get your men geared up, pick more men from the cavalry units waiting outside for orders, and be on your way."

"Yes, General. I should be ready to leave in another hour or two." With that, Tarleton left the general to complete his plans for the invasion of North Carolina.

As Tarleton left the general's tent, he did not notice a young Tory, by the name of Will, slipping away from the back of the tent where the window was located. He did not see this same young man scurry across the field to the horse pasture, nor observe him hastily grab a horse from the corral. Nor did the sentries stop him as he galloped South in the direction of the Santee and Snow Island, for he was well-known by all as a loyal British citizen waiting for the rebels to be defeated. But how wrong they were!

Will waved at the sentries as he flew by them on Saucy, his chestnut-colored mare. She was a strong little horse and could run steadily for some time before getting tired. She was from good stock, Will reasoned, and would carry him faithfully to his destination on Snow Island. He was thinking about how successful his first spying mission had been and how this would prove to Marion that he could be trusted as a member of Marion's militia.

Colonel Marion would be so proud of him, and he, a so-called Tory! He had given up Tory politics and switched sides when he saw how his own people, as well as Americans fighting for their independence, were being treated by the British officers and their minions. Their brutish behavior was unacceptable!

He had accidentally come upon Marion and his band near Benbow's Ferry, where the colonel and his men had established a secure defensible position against the British. Marion's guards found him outside of the encampment, and, thinking that he was spying on them, took him immediately to their commander. Will had heard much about the militia leader but had never seen or met him, and he was taken aback by the inoffensive-looking man in front of him. He surely did not look like the man about whom he had heard so much!

He smiled to himself when he thought of how Colonel Tarleton continually complained about this ghost who hid out in the swamps. However, like Thomas, he wiped the smile from his face when Marion spoke. His voice had been neither wimpy nor delicate. His words to Will were hard, firm, and solid, and made the hair stand up on the back of his arms and neck.

"What are you doing here? You are dressed like a Tory! Who sent you? What do you want? What is your business in this area?" Marion harshly questioned.

"I am sorry, Sir. I just blundered into your location, not meaning to. I was actually looking for you, if you are Colonel Francis Marion. I want to join up with you. I am tired of the devastation that is caused by my own people, the Tories and British soldiers. I am ready to change sides. Can you use me?"

"Well, now. How can I trust you? We are a very close-knit group here, and outsiders are welcome, but they must prove themselves."

"What must I do to prove myself, Colonel?"

"How old are you, young man? By the way, what is your name?"

"Will. Actually, William Francis, Sir. I am seventeen years old, and my family owns a small plantation here in the South Carolina lowlands. I have thrown off my family's Tory politics, so my parents disinherited me and sent me on my way. They are staunch supporters of the British government, and would not countenance having a 'traitor' to their cause in their midst. I am happy to be out on my own, believing what I want, and not what is being forced upon me."

"Don't get me wrong, Sir. My parents are good people and I still love them, but they are being hornswoggled by the British leadership. So, I am here to serve, Colonel Marion, wherever you can use me."

"You are well-known to the British, then, Will?"

"Yes, Sir, I am. They know me because I have been to Cornwallis's camp many times with my father. I have made friends with many of the fusiliers. The cavalrymen are fond of my horse, Saucy, a sweet little mare who can outdistance all of their horses. So, yes, they know me well."

As Will was speaking, Marion had an indecipherable look on his face. Thomas, who was standing close to him, knew what he was thinking. Hadn't they just had a discussion about spying for General Greene just a few days before? Thomas could almost see the wheels turning in Marion's brain. Here was an opportunity for them to garner information about the activities of the British! He was so deep in thought that he was startled when Marion began speaking again.

Colonel Marion looked over his shoulder at Thomas but called out to his second-in-command, Major John James. He also called over the Horry brothers, Peter and Hugh, as well as some of the men who had been with him the longest, including Buddy, his servant. "Come join me, men. I have an idea pounding in my head. See if it makes any sense to you, and if it has any merit to it at all." As Thomas seemed to be included in the discussion with the other men, he nonchalantly joined in as they all walked to a clearing away from the rest of the band who continued to stand on guard, watching the newcomer, Will.

"Here's what I'm thinking. We have this young upstart named Will, who seems to have an in with the British. What if we give him the opportunity to prove himself by sending him back into Cornwallis's camp to gather the information that General Greene urgently needs?"

Chapter 6

"How do you know you can trust him, Colonel?" Major James asked. "He knows where to find us if he changes his mind and squeals to the British. Colonel Tarleton would be down on us like a tick on a British bulldog. They already know that you are headquartered here on Snow Island."

"That's true, John, but they don't know that we have several locations here in the swamp that we use as a base for operations," countered the colonel. "With our sentries posted everywhere, we would know their whereabouts at all times. So, what say you, men? Do you think it could work?"

Thomas wanted to say something but what could he say to all the experienced men standing around him. After all, he was only a fifteen-year-old kid and he didn't have any knowledge about spying or warfare at all. But, he decided to put his thoughts into the equation as well. "Colonel, I think it's a good idea. I could even go with him part of the way, so that he would have company, and know that there would be one of your band keeping an eye on him. Not that I have the expertise or know-how that you all have."

"Fine idea, Thomas," Marion stated. "I would not want you to go into the British camp, though, just in case Will is not as trustworthy as we may think. We don't want you taken and held prisoner. Luke and Jonas will go a short distance with you both and then they will stop along the way. You and Will shall continue to a further point, at which place you will wait for him to return from his information-gathering mission. Then you both will return together, catching up with Luke and Jonas who will then bring you back safely. Now, to discuss this plan with Will."

"All right, Will," stated Marion. Gaining the boy's attention, Marion continued, "Here's what's going to happen. You want to prove that you are being sincere about joining my brigade, so here is your opportunity to do that. You say that you are familiar with Cornwallis's camp, so I'm going to send you back there for some much-needed information." Marion then told Will of the plan and that Thomas, Luke, and Jonas would accompany him so far. "Do you think that you can do that without being caught?"

At that point, Will had responded with a "Yes, Sir!"

So, now, here he was flying back to meet up with the other members of the band who awaited him a few miles away. He had completed what Marion had asked him to do and he breathed a sigh of relief that he was able to get cleanly away. He could now return with Thomas, Luke, and Jonas back to Snow Island. He smiled to himself about a job well done.

As all four riders galloped into camp, Marion limped forward, anxious to hear what the boy had learned on his spying quest. Before the horses came to a complete stop, Thomas and Will were off them, racing toward the colonel, excited about their first spying mission. Although Thomas did not actually do any of the spying, he was thrilled to be any part of this information process.

Will could barely contain himself. "Sir, I found out what you and general Greene want to know." He proceeded to explain what he had heard in Cornwallis's camp about the new recruits, where and which way they would be traveling, and that they would be escorted to their final destination by a cavalry unit. From there, they would become a part of Cornwallis's army heading into North Carolina.

Marion was so energized by this news that he almost did a little jig. He quickly sent off a letter to General Greene by his swiftest horseman, explaining what their spy work had uncovered. In the letter, Marion told the general that his militia would interfere in the plans of the British and give the new recruits a good scare.

Upon receiving the letter from Marion, Greene decided to leave everything in Marion's hands, since there would be no time for a return message from him.

By this time, Marion's small brigade had become large enough to take care of the two hundred new recruits. When he learned, through other Whig sympathizers, that the fledgling soldiers would be marching to a slow drumbeat to Camden, Marion decided to let them know he was in the area. He and his brigade quickly caught up with the infantry, and his riflemen opened fire on the pickets who had been guarding the rear of the main column of soldiers.

"Surround them, men!" Marion called out. "Cover the front and the flank. Don't let them get away!" Since Marion's troops were mounted, they were able to stop the forward movement of the British regulars. When his troops swung around, and gunfire occurred, several of the British soldiers were killed or wounded. The British were on foot, and they were at a definite disadvantage, causing the panicked recruits to dash into an open field, and hide behind trees and fences.

As soon as their scare tactics ended, and confusion reigned within the ranks of the British soldiers, Marion withdrew his men. He circled his horse around the brigade asking, "Is everyone safe? Any injuries?" When he received light-hearted responses for the most part, he decided to spend the night watching the British, who had already lit their campfires at a safe distance from the rebels. Crossing the road, Marion called Luke and Jonas to set up sentries around their camp for the night. Everyone settled down for a much-needed rest and thought no more of shooting at the enemy, at least for this day.

In the meantime, the British commander, Robert McLeroth, entrusted with getting these new recruits to Cornwallis in a timely manner, wanted to avoid another fighting engagement with Colonel Marion and his militia, so before dawn on the following morning, he slipped away with his recruits before Marion knew that he was gone.

The next morning, when Marion was notified by Major James that the British had silently retreated during the night, Marion laughed and said, "Well, men, it appears that I have been outfoxed this time! But, that will be a fight for another day. According to the major here, McLeroth has left all of his supply wagons and heavy equipment behind, and we can make good use of those spoils of war. Let's get it hauled away before he sends troops back to retrieve it."

Thomas was relieved that they would be on their way back to the camp. He was glad that the British had moved on because he did not want to be engaged in another fight with them. He didn't know if he could actually fire at or kill another man, but if the colonel gave the order to fire, he would have to follow through.

Will walked up to him at that point and asked, "What are you thinking, Thomas?"

He responded, "I'm glad that I don't have to shoot at anyone this morning!"

"Me, too," said Will. "Like you, most of my shooting has been at wild animals out in the woods behind our plantation. Even though I'm seventeen, I have not been an avid rifleman, but if Colonel Marion needs me to do just that, I will."

"I guess we had better hurry and help these men get those supply wagons home," said Thomas. "Wow! I never thought that I would refer to a swamp as home, but that's what it is for now. Are you going to stay with us, Will?"

"Well, since I've been kicked out of my own home until this war is over, I guess I don't really have a choice. I can either stay here and help fight, or wander around by myself, which isn't really a pleasant option for me. I want to be where I can help the cause however I can."

"I wonder what the colonel's new plans are. I know that this spying will continue but I also understand that we have to do our part in driving those Redcoats out of South Carolina," Thomas said.

"All I'm wondering about, right now," shivered Will, "is how long it's going to take us to get back to the camp. It is getting downright cold around here and I would love to feel the warmth of that fire pit, right about now. I am so glad that Colonel Marion has established that secret lair as his main hideout on Snow Island. At least it's a place where we can rest and warm up, as well as a place where we can rendezvous."

As the colony of men, supply wagons, and equipment headed back to Snow Island, a messenger passed them, heading as fast as possible on the rugged road. Upon seeing Colonel Marion ahead of him, he quickly drew his horse to a halt and slipped out of the saddle. As out of breath as his horse, the rider raced over to Marion, still mounted on his own horse, and gasped, "Colonel, I have a message for you from General Greene. It is of the utmost importance that you respond immediately, so that the general can know your plans!"

Since Thomas had arrived with the first message, Marion had received several letters from the general telling him how to work out his own ideas. He sometimes was irritated with instructions that were so different from his own. He basically trusted his own instincts, so it was no surprise to him that Greene wanted to know his upcoming plans.

Knowing that the Continentals and militia needed to work together to succeed, he decided that the first thing to do would be to let the general know that the new recruits had received their first glimpse of the Swamp Fox, and they had been terrified! Now, he had better look at this new missive from the general to see what was required of him in the near future.

Chapter 7

Three days later, Cornwallis stormed around in his headquarters. "How on earth did that man learn about the recruits?" He thundered. "He ambushed us again! Marion is a menace! We have got to get rid of him somehow!" He roared. "Does he have spies everywhere in South Carolina? He simply has to be stopped, and stopped now!"

Colonel Tarleton, unfortunately, was the one receiving the brunt of the general's outcry. He was afraid that the British commander was going to have a stroke, his face was so purple! He put his brain in gear, trying to come up with some solution to the general's dilemma. "Since he seemingly has spies all over, why don't we do the same thing, Sir? Maybe, we could get one of our own men into Marion's tight militia. It might be difficult because Marion will be wary of any new person trying to join his band, but I think that I have come up with a way to do it."

"How so?" Cornwallis asked. "We know that his numbers are not as high as ours, yet he seems to outfight us at every turn."

"Here's my idea, Sir. My sergeant has lived in the colonies for a few years now and knows the people pretty well. He could fit in easily as a colonial and could probably convince someone to help him join the band."

"I'm not sure that would work but I like your idea. Let's push it a little farther. Instead of finding someone to take him there, why don't we rough him up a little and drop him somewhere close to the swamp that protects Marion and his men? Marion's men would find him injured and the sergeant could explain that he had come across a small detail of British cavalry, and they had beaten him."

"That's good, General. I think that would work better. If you want to follow through with this suggestion, I'll go right now and talk with Sergeant Durham. I'm sure he would go along with the idea, especially if we give him a bonus in his pay for taking the risk to spy for us."

Later, the next evening, a bruised and bloodied sergeant was dropped off near Snow Island, where he waited for someone to rescue him; hopefully, someone from Marion's band.

Luke and Jonas leisurely poked along as they patrolled the area just outside the swamp. "What do you think about our new recruit, Will?" Jonas asked. "Do you think he will fit in, especially since he is highly educated and grew up on a wealthy plantation? This type of life may not suit him—scrounging around for food and ammunition as we have to often do."

"Well, he did bring the colonel information that he needed concerning those new recruits," Luke answered.

Jonas had been looking down and around them as they walked along, noting who or what might be in the shadows. He lifted his head and squinted as his eyes adjusted to the lack of light that had slowly changed the swampy region into a gloomy bog. His eyes suddenly glanced upon something in the roadway ahead. "Hey, Luke! What's that in the path up ahead? It looks like a person. Let's check it out."

"Okay, but let's be cautious. You never know, during this war, what or who might be lurking around," responded Luke.

As the guys got closer to the clump in the middle of the road, they could see that the blob, which was indistinguishable from a distance, was actually a man in worn, torn, and dirty clothes. His face was somewhat disfigured by the blood that was drying on his face and hairline, so that Luke and Jonas could not tell if this man was known to them.

"What a mess! What happened to him? How did he get this close without us knowing that he was here? We need to take him to the camp and help him," stated Jonas. "This man has been well-and-truly beaten," he continued. "We need to report him to the colonel. It's unfortunate that our doctor had to leave because of an emergency at home, but maybe Buddy can doctor him. You know that he sometimes assists the physician with his patients."

"All this man seems to need is to have his cuts and bruises cleaned up, anyway. Luke, why don't you round up his horse? I think I saw it chomping on the grass near here," Jonas said.

Upon procuring the stranger's ride, Luke said, "Okay, mister, on your feet. I'm sorry, but we must lead you blindfolded to our camp. It's merely a matter of precaution." The middle-aged man nodded his head in understanding as Jonas prepared to tie a scarf around the man's eyes. "Okay, here's your horse. Give me your left foot and I'll fit it into the stirrup. Now swing yourself over and sit in the saddle. I'll lead your horse. You just hold on. Do you think you can manage to sit in the saddle without falling off?" Luke asked.

The man, who had not said one word during this whole interchange, simply nodded his head in agreement. Though he spoke not a word, his swollen eyes had been taking in everything they could see before he had been blindfolded. He had looked at the two roughshod men who were helping him. They certainly did not appear to be a part of any organized group of men that could run the British around like Marion was doing.

They wore no uniform, their clothing being just homespun. They did have white feathers in their caps, but that meant nothing to him. Maybe they were just two good Samaritans helping him. But, if that was the case, why was he now blindfolded? Anyway, he was glad to have been found. Now, he could, hopefully, carry out the mission given to him by Tarleton.

After a couple of grueling hours, sitting blindfolded in the saddle, the men finally stopped and helped him down off his horse. They removed the scarf from his eyes, and as he adjusted to the dim light, all he could see was the swamp, and not much more. If there were a hideout here, he would never be able to find it. Make no wonder he and the other British soldiers had not been able to locate it. He knew that the soldiers would never spend so much time looking for this camp. But, where, exactly, was the camp? He couldn't tell.

Luke gently nudged him forward. "Step carefully, now," he said. "You never know what you might step on. All kinds of creatures live here, not just two-legged ones."

I must be near the camp, he thought.

Jonas had stopped in front of him and let out the call of a loon. It was different from the whip-poor-will call and a loon call combined. The fact that Jonas had only made the loon's call alerted the sentries that they were coming, but were unsure of the person they were leading—whether friend or foe. This reminded the men to be wary of what they said or did in the stranger's presence. Of course, the man they were leading would not be aware of the change in calls, whatsoever.

He would think that it was just a signal that part of Marion's band had returned to the hideout. After giving the loon call, Luke removed the wounded man's blindfold, and told him again to watch his step as they neared the camp.

Up ahead, the sergeant saw the first sign of life—a huge fire pit surrounded by a number of ill-clothed men. Again, no uniforms were in sight! As the three of them neared the fire, his face became illuminated by the flames. Everyone could see his bloodied face and torn clothes now. Hopefully, he was not recognizable to anyone here. To make himself more pitiable, he stumbled purposely to the ground. He had to look like a beaten man, so that the band would believe his story. He still hadn't spoken a word to Luke and Jonas in all this time.

Luke quickly went to his side and called out, "This man is in need of doctoring. Is Buddy around? We could use his help. Where is Buddy, anyhow? He's the only one here who can help him."

The sergeant's eyes widened, as much as they could, when a burly black man came over and knelt beside him. The sergeant tried to back away from the man.

"No need to fear, Sir. I'm the colonel's personal servant and have some knowledge of doctoring. Let me take a look at you. You look like you got quite a bad beating, what with all the mess of blood on your face and clothes. Your right eye could use a poultice to bring down the swelling, and your scratches are rather deep. They may even scar but I'll do my best to not let that happen. You just sit here a while and I'll go and get what I need to fix you up."

The sergeant nodded his head and closed his eyes. His fellow soldiers had really done a good job on him if he looked as bad as he felt. There should be no doubt that he had been viciously pummeled.

When Buddy returned with his supplies, the sergeant tried to muster up a smile for the servant. He tried not to wince while the scrapes and scratches were cleaned, but when the poultice was applied to his eye, he nearly jumped out of his skin. The first words out of his mouth for several hours were, "Ouch! That stings!"

"You'll be fine," Buddy snickered. "It only stings for a short while and then the swelling will go down fast." He continued his tender care by putting a bandage on the man's head to help keep the dressing in place.

When Buddy had finished taking care of his cuts, the sergeant became aware of another man standing over him. He looked up to see a short man, dressed somewhat like an officer, staring down at him. Turning away from the sergeant, the man shifted and looked at his men and asked, "Who is this stranger in our camp?"

Luke and Jonas both answered at the same time. "We don't know, Sir. We couldn't get anything out of him. It was like he was in a daze and had lost his ability to think or even speak. Maybe now that he feels better, he can offer an explanation of how he came to be in the middle of the road, so close to Snow

Island. Obviously, he was attacked by someone or something. His horse was still nearby, and knowing that you wouldn't want us to leave him without giving him any help, we loaded him on his horse and brought him here."

"We did blindfold him, Colonel, so that he wouldn't be able to find his way back again, should he need to leave. We're sorry for making such a brash and ill-advised decision. On second thought, we could have taken him to an inn that wasn't too far away. But again, we would have had to leave our post unguarded to do that."

Marion glanced at the stranger, who at this point posed no threat to the camp. "I would like to question this man as soon as he is able to get up on two legs. Bring him to my quarters within the half hour."

"Yes, Sir," replied his men.

Standing just a little way from the colonel and the stranger, Thomas and Will had heard the request of the colonel. Will leaned over and whispered in Thomas's ear, "That man seems very familiar to me but I can't figure out where I have seen him before. Do you know him, Thomas?"

Thomas responded, "No, but I agree with you that there is something about him that makes me nervous. I just don't know what it is. Maybe it will come to both of us before too long. Perhaps, we should inform the colonel that there is something about this person that produces a little anxiety in us. We should talk to him now before he hears what that man has to say."

"I'm with you. Let's go," said Will.

As the two young men, who were also new to this brigade, approached the colonel's quarters, they could hear him speaking with the Horry brothers, Peter and Hugh. "Men," he said, "what do you make of this stranger? You two are great judges of character, and I rely on you with any decision I make concerning him. He hasn't told us his story, yet, and maybe we should hold our judgment until later. What do you think?"

Hugh answered and said, "We don't know this man. He is not familiar to us and does not live in the area. Otherwise, we would have met him at some point. Do you think he could be a plant by the British to find out about our location? But, you're right, Colonel. I think that we need to talk to him first."

Thomas and Will had overheard the conversation, and looking at each other, decided that this would be the time to talk to the colonel, while his seconds-in-command were with him. Hesitantly, Thomas cleared his throat and called out to their leader. "Colonel Marion, Sir, Will and I would like to have a word with you concerning this stranger in our camp. May we speak with you?"

"Come on in, boys. What is it that you need me to hear about our guest out there?" He looked from one to the other and then raised his brows in question.

Will spoke first, but slowly. As he was the newest member of this group, he didn't want to upset his commander by making any false accusations against the stranger. "I think that I know this man. I have seen him somewhere but I can't remember when or where. Most of my time has been spent on the plantation or with my father when he was with the British officers."

"And what about you, Thomas?" The commander asked. "What do you know about this man?"

"Nothing pertinent, Sir. He just made me nervous with the way he was watching you and everyone else around him. I couldn't tell you exactly what it is about him that makes me feel that way."

Marion looked askance at the Horry brothers. "Let's give him an hour or two to start feeling better, and then I will question him about his business in this area. Then we'll go from there. Thanks, boys, for bringing your feelings about him to my attention. You are dismissed, but keep your eyes on him until we know more about him."

Thomas and Will exited the colonel's quarters and walked toward the firepit. There they sat and continued whispering together, trying to figure out what made them so leery about this stranger in the camp.

Chapter 8

In the meantime, Sergeant Durham assumed he was in the main headquarters of the Swamp Fox, and was wondering how he could safely get back to General Cornwallis and let him know the size of this brigade, where it was likely located, and how they could break it apart. He kept an eye on everyone's position and tried to come up with an excuse to leave and get back to his own regiment. Of course, he had been blindfolded and really did not know how he got here, but he guessed that he could find a path out if he had to leave on his own.

Buddy had done a good job fixing him up and the poultice on his eye was causing the swelling to go down, allowing him to have full use of both eyes. He stealthily stretched the muscles in his arms and legs, not wanting anyone to notice that he was sturdier than they thought.

Colonel Marion's eyes seemed to look right through him when he had studied him earlier. Durham knew that his story would have to be good because it looked like this man could even read his thoughts and know what his full story was. Make no wonder they were having such a hard time trying to catch him! He appeared to be quite cunning. The sergeant didn't think much could get by this man. As he was thinking this, the colonel, himself, walked out of his quarters and headed toward him. It looked like now was the time to give him a story about being where they found him.

"So, how are you feeling now, friend? Are you able to tell us about yourself and how you got beaten up? What is your name and from where do you hail?"

The sergeant put as much pain into his answer as he could, and responded. "I am George Kilcannon, and I was on my way to Charlestown to visit a sick cousin. I was riding along, minding my own business, when a small unit of British soldiers came out of nowhere and attacked me. I'm just a country farmer from farther North, and I tried to explain that to them. I told them what my destination was and why I was going there, but they chose to ignore my explanation."

"Instead, they beat me and left me for dead in the scrub by the side of the road. I managed to crawl to the middle of the road before I blacked out, and that's apparently where your men found me. From their comments, they thought I might be one of your men, and I assume that I am now looking at Colonel Francis Marion."

"You are, Sir. I'm sorry you've come to such a sorry pass, but I will leave you now, so that you can rest up some more. We'll speak again later."

The colonel sauntered back to his quarters, motioning to Peter and Hugh as he did so. At the same time, Thomas started walking toward the colonel, but not too rapidly, so as not to gain the attention of George Kilcannon, if that were his real name.

"Colonel," Thomas whispered. "I knew that he was familiar. If I hadn't heard him talking to you, I would not have realized that I had heard his voice before. Do you recollect what I had told you about how I had run into a British cavalry unit before I got to this camp?"

"Yes, I remember, Thomas."

"Well, Colonel, that's the sergeant I heard speaking to Colonel Tarleton and complaining that you were too hard to find. I'm sure of it!"

"Are you quite certain of this, Thomas?"

"As sure as my name is Thomas Sinclair, Sir!"

"All right, Thomas. I'll look into this, and if what you say is true, we will take care of this untimely visitor." Saying that, he dismissed Thomas and continued on to his quarters. Peter and Hugh followed quickly behind. "Okay, men. Thomas just enlightened me about our guest out there. He is definitely not who he says he is. According to Thomas, that man is actually a sergeant and part of Tarleton's cavalry and has been sent here to spy on us."

"But, Sir, is Thomas sure that he's right about this man?" Peter asked.

"I trust Thomas's judgment on this, Peter. He was quite adamant about what he said. Thomas is a smart young man, maybe not too experienced, but I believe what he says. So, let's think on this conundrum and see what kind of cheese we can put into the mousetrap that's going to catch our interloper."

"Yes, Sir." Both brothers answered at the same time because they were all of the same mind. Protection at any cost!

Marion walked over to his desk and picked up a letter that he had recently received from General Greene. Looking at it carefully, he smiled and said, "I think we have our cheese, boys, and a way to flummox Tarleton."

"I have been wondering how to respond to this letter from Greene, and now I think I have the perfect solution to not only get rid of our unwelcome guest, but to follow through with General Greene's plans for our brigade."

Just as he finished speaking, a knock sounded on the door of his quarters.

Marion sent Hugh to see who was there. He returned and told the colonel that Thomas was at the door and wanted to speak to him. "Well, let him in, then. Let's see what other information he can give us."

"I'm sorry for interrupting again, Sir, but Will and I would like to help when you come to a decision about the sergeant out there. His eyes are still roaming and he appears to be conniving about something. We really don't trust him. He is just acting too suspiciously!"

"Okay, Thomas. I will keep you and Will in mind if and when we decide what to do with the sergeant." The boys both left to go back and keep an eye on Kilcannon.

"As I was saying, gents, let's just go along with Kilcannon's story, allowing him to believe that we are on his side and commiserate with him about the ordeal he has faced. If we don't appear overly cautious around him, maybe he will relax and let his guard down."

"Now, here's what I'm thinking. General Greene has arrived in Charlotte, North Carolina, where he hopes to delay Cornwallis's advance into that colony. He is dividing his forces, even though his army in the South is not overly large. He will be leading the main American force Southeast and we will be assisting Daniel Morgan in defending the Western part of South Carolina. We will essentially be continuing to do what we have been doing up to this point: keeping this area free of Tory control and making sure that Tarleton and his cavalry are stymied at every point."

"Let's go out and gather our men around us. We will work out the details with them which will help us to achieve our objective. In the meantime, we will allow Kilcannon close enough to hear what our plans are."

"But, Colonel," complained Hugh, "he will know what we are doing and tell the British."

"That's the sweet part of this, Hugh. Our real plans will not be discussed near him, so he will only learn of our counterfeit scheme. In other words, we will conspire to trick the enemy with a counterplan. But I need to get the major on board with our game plan. He should be arriving back to camp shortly."

"I like it," said Hugh. "Our goal here is to outsmart the spy in our camp!"

"Correct," said the colonel as he led the brothers outside.

While they were walking toward the small group of militiamen, who were close by, Major James approached in a hurry. He stepped down from his horse and tossed the reins at Simon. "Wipe him down well, Simon! We have been galloping at a good speed to get here with urgent news."

"Yes, Major," responded Simon. "I will also feed and water him."

Major James hailed the colonel and asked that they speak together, alone. The two men hustled off to the colonel's quarters where they had the needed privacy for the discussion.

"What is it, John?" Marion asked. "What news do you have that is so pressing?"

"I have two pieces of information to give to you, Sir. I think, first of all, you will be pleased to know that there will be a letter coming to you soon from Governor Rutledge. He has commissioned you as a brigadier-general in the South Carolina militia with authority over the Lowcountry. You are now the senior and most active militia commander in this part of South Carolina. Congratulations, General!"

"Well, well! Thank you for that great news, John. I will continue to do my best for the war effort, especially here in South Carolina. I hope to see the governor soon and thank him in person." On hearing that he had just become a general, Marion continued his questioning of the major, as if increasing in rank was not that important. "So, what is your second piece of news, John?"

"I am not as happy to impart the second part of the news, Sir. You know that the Battle of Camden was a near disaster for us. Cornwallis really whipped the militias and the Continentals there, and as a result, the British have almost subjugated the whole of South Carolina. If it hadn't been for you and our militia, we would be under their control right now. The news that is sadder is that most of the casualties of this whole revolution have been right here in South Carolina."

"I fear that it will be worse before this war has ended. We have lost many of our own militia during our campaigns, and I hope and pray, as you do, Sir, that we can soon end these hostilities!"

"I, too, am saddened that we have lost so many warriors, many of whom were just young men ready to start their lives. If I could snap my fingers to end this war, I would gladly do so. In the meantime, however, we have our own questionable situation in this camp. We have a spy sitting right out there, who probably is wondering what we are talking about. Through young Thomas, we have learned that he is a sergeant in Colonel Tarleton's cavalry of dragoons. Peter and Hugh Horry and I had just been discussing this before your arrival."

Marion told John that he had been waiting for him to return, so that he could get his take on the plan before it was carried out. As he explained his plan to the major, John kept nodding his head in agreement as to what the general wanted to do. "I agree with your decision wholeheartedly, Sir. Let's put it into motion as soon as possible."

"My thoughts exactly, John. So, let's go out and get our men geared up." As they wandered nonchalantly back to the band, Marion wondered if their plan could actually work. A lot could go wrong. How would they let the sergeant get away? How would they know that he delivered the false information? Could any of his men get hurt in the process? In his opinion, he had already lost too many men during his time as the militia leader in South Carolina. He didn't want to put them in further jeopardy if his idea did not work.

As they neared the watchful men, Marion noticed that Thomas and Will were being very vigilant in keeping their eyes on the spy. He motioned to his brigade to gather around him. Thomas and Will joined the company surrounding the colonel, keeping their eyes ever alert for any movement from the sergeant. The colonel intentionally strolled closer to the spy, so that the sergeant could clearly hear what was being discussed.

"Men, we have a new mission. Listen closely to what I say because this will be an important engagement, and the war effort may hinge on what we do during this time. As usual, we are fighting two enemies, the Redcoats and their Tory supporters. We have to be very careful to keep our plans silent as there are many Tory spies around."

"So, what's the plan, Colonel?" Luke asked.

Major James spoke up before Marion could answer, and said, "First, men, there is something important that you should know. Our Colonel Marion is now Brigadier-General Marion. He was recently promoted by Governor Rutledge. Let's give our good 'General' a hearty hurrah, shall we?"

The men enthusiastically cheered and clapped their hands, showing their beloved commander their total loyalty to his leadership. Huzzahs and hoorays abounded throughout the camp. Even the sergeant half-heartedly threw in a cheer. After all, he had to make it appear that he was a loyal Patriot…

"Okay, men. I appreciate your response to the news, but now it is time to get our plan put together. General Greene wants us to assist in the attack of Fort Ninety-Six. Any and all ideas will be considered."

"We have been informed that we will join General Morgan's forces at Ninety-Six in Western South Carolina. It is an important British fortified village held by about five hundred and fifty Loyalists. Daniel Morgan's plans are to take that fort by the end of January. We will be on hand to assist him in whatever way he requires. We will meet up with him in one week, and hopefully oust those Tories from Ninety-Six."

"Excuse me, Sir, but where is Ninety-Six?" Thomas asked. "It seems to be a funny name for a town. As you know, I am new to this area and many of the towns have astonishing names, even more so than in New England."

Colonel Marion answered, "The town of Ninety-Six, Thomas, was established in 1730 at the crossroads of an important trade route. It got its strange name from traders who believed it was 96 miles to the nearest Cherokee settlement of Keowee, where they traded with the natives living there."

"Now that I understand the reasoning for its name, it doesn't sound quite so strange," laughed Thomas.

"Okay, boys, let's get moving. We have a lot of things to do before we join General Morgan at Ninety-Six," yelled out Major James.

Chapter 9

Sergeant Durham couldn't believe his ears! They were discussing their plans right in front of him. How lucky could he be! *Now, if I could just get away from here and report to General Cornwallis, I will be lauded for helping advance the British cause in the colonies,* he thought. *I'll just have to wait and see what will be happening here that will help me escape.* He wasn't tied up, so that would not hinder his getting away. *They must have believed my story; otherwise, I would not have been left on my own all of the time that I've been here. They actually think that I am a loyal Patriot. I must be a great actor!*

As the spy watched all of the goings on around him, he silently devised a plan in his mind that might work in his favor. He could feign continued illness from being beaten up, thereby staying behind while everyone went ahead. Or, he could simply stay at the end of the line, and slip away when no one was watching. It would really help if they trusted him with a musket or pistol, but he was sure that wouldn't be happening.

In the meantime, Marion's band of men was scuttling around gathering all of their needed articles: guns, ammunition, food, blankets, water, and medicine. Durham watched as the men enumerated all of the items and then checked off everything on their lists.

Major James hollered out, "Take as much as you will need, men, as we don't know how long we will be required to stay during this rendezvous with General Morgan."

"Yes, Sir," replied the men.

"And make sure your horses are in a healthy condition," the major reminded them. "Check their hooves and their shoes to make sure they can carry you and any added weight. We don't want any split hooves or horseshoes flying around causing your mounts to limp."

The major turned his attention to Kilcannon. "Hey, you, Kilcannon! Do you know how to saddle a horse and use a firearm?"

"Absolutely, Sir!" Kilcannon responded. He was glad that he would have a horse and a musket. What more could he ask for? *Escape just got a whole lot easier,* he mused.

The Horry brothers passed among the men, encouraging them to speedily finish their packing, and then get some sleep for they would be leaving early on the morrow. "Get some sack time in as soon as you can, boys," called out Hugh to the men. "We leave at sun-up. Buddy will have breakfast waiting for you, so get up early enough to eat. You will need the added nourishment before the day is over!"

Early the next morning, everyone, including Thomas and Will, was already in his saddle, ready to go. Even Ebony was chomping at the bit, hoping to be able to take a good gallop since he hadn't been released from the pasture for several days. Thomas crooned softly, reassuring him that they would be moving out soon. Beside him, Will fidgeted on his horse.

While both boys knew that this engagement would not entail any fighting, per se, he, like Thomas, had never been in this position before. Here they were with a spy in the camp, having to pretend they were going to engage the enemy in battle. It was a little nerve-wracking to say the least!

The men would be riding single file through the swamp. Luke and Simon had been given their positions the night before by Colonel Marion. They were to ride at the end of the line with their spy, Mr. Kilcannon. At some point of the trip, they were to pretend to become distracted by something in order to give Kilcannon an opportunity to escape.

Not everyone was happy about letting the sergeant go, but this was Marion's plan, and they would follow through. Hopefully, the counterfeit plan would make its way back to Cornwallis and he would have to change his itinerary to move his troops away from North Carolina again.

An hour after leaving camp, something in the underbrush claimed Lucas's and Simon's attention. Lucas proceeded to pass the other riders and raced to the front of the line to inform Colonel Marion that something suspicious was noticed in the underbrush, possibly a red uniform. While Lucas was riding toward the colonel, Simon took off in the opposite direction. This left Kilcannon alone at the end of the file. Several horses separated him from the nearest soldier, so he thought that this would be his chance to disappear from sight.

Kilcannon slowed his horse to a walk, causing more distance to grow between him and the rest of the band. Making as little noise as possible, he casually turned his horse in a different direction. He headed to the East of the line of men, hoping that he would, somehow, find his way out of the swamp. Sure enough, there was a rarely-traveled path that he soon came upon.

He rode his horse cautiously, fearing that the rest of the men would hear his horse's hooves as they traversed the twigs and leaves scattered on the trail. He knew that it might take several hours, or even a day, to get back to Cornwallis's camp, so he had to go as speedily as possible, yet keep the noise level down. It would be unthinkable, now, to get caught, as Marion would surely recognize the fact that he had been a spy amidst them.

Marion would probably have him hanged at this point, especially after treating him like one of the militia. Fear raced up and down his spine at the thought and gave him a large amount of unrest. "I must reach safety and get back to the British lines as quickly as I can," he muttered under his breath.

In the meantime, Simon had returned to the end of the line where he had left the spy. As he thought, Kilcannon wasn't there waiting for him. At the same time, Lucas returned, having told the colonel what was happening. Marion had sent him back and told him to pretend that nothing had happened, for quite often, men would leave the brigade and go home without telling anyone.

Knowing that Kilcannon had swallowed the bait, Lucas and Simon continued in a lively conversation about what they may have seen by the side of the road. Of course, this would be just acting, in case the spy was still close by and could hear them.

After Lucas had given the colonel the message about Kilcannon's opportunity to escape, Major James rode his horse up to Marion and asked, "What do we do now, Colonel? It seems as if our spy has taken off with a plan that will surely frustrate Cornwallis."

"We'll continue on to Daniel Morgan's camp, and see how we can assist him, before returning to Snow Island," Marion replied.

Chapter 10

"Ho, the camp!" The picket yelled. "Rider coming! Pretty fast, too! It looks to be one of our own! It's Sergeant Durham but he's out of uniform! Where has he been?"

Durham galloped into the British camp and threw himself off his horse as he raced toward General Cornwallis's headquarters. "General, General Cornwallis!" He called. "There's going to be a battle at Fort Ninety-Six! We need to hurry and get there before Marion and his men! On top of that, I know how the headquarters of the Swamp Fox is set up, and quite possibly how to find his nest. I just escaped from his men and they are on their way to attack Fort Ninety-Six, Sir!"

"Hold on, Durham, slow down! Explain to me everything you have heard and seen. Then, we will discuss Fort Ninety-Six."

"Well, Sir. The ruse worked as we had hoped. They discovered me beaten up on the roadside and took me to their camp, where I met all the men and the Swamp Fox himself. They believed my story about being jumped and mercilessly flogged by British soldiers. The wounds that the soldiers gave me proved to them that it was so. There were only about twenty men there, so I feel that his brigade is not as large as we thought."

"What's more, I now know why we could never find them. The area is so secluded that you would need a road map to find your way there."

"The question is this, Sergeant. Do you think you could find your way back?" Tarleton asked.

"Even though I was blindfolded during the trip to Marion's headquarters, I think that I could find my way back if need be. Will you invade his camp while he is absent from it, Colonel?"

"I need to think about this plot to invade Fort Ninety-Six first, Sergeant, before I make any decisions about what to do. Thank you for the information and for getting back to our camp in time to take advantage of the upcoming situation at the fort. You have done well, and you will find a bonus in your next pay pouch." General Cornwallis dismissed Sergeant Durham, and he turned to Tarleton. "What do you recommend, Banastre?"

"Losing Fort Ninety-Six to the Colonials would harm our hold on South Carolina, Sir, but it is also tempting to outfox the Fox while he is away from his lair. Do you think we could do both at the same time, General?"

"I don't see why not," responded Cornwallis. "I could take a small group of fusiliers with me to stop Marion before he gets to the fort, while you take apart his headquarters. If Durham is right, and Marion has only a few men, we could manage it with a detachment from the regiment without hindering our strength here at my headquarters."

"That sounds like a good plan, General. When should we start out?"

"The day is almost gone, so this would not be a good time to leave. After all, there are rebels roaming around and we don't want to be their prey at night. I think that we must prepare our men for the journey and start out at dawn tomorrow. Go now and make plans with Major Poole, whom we'll put in charge of this detachment. Tell him that we will prepare for battle within the next few days, so he should plan his provisions accordingly. You, also, will need to be ready to leave at a moment's notice for your own excursion into the Swamp Fox's headquarters."

"Yes, Sir. I will do so immediately," responded the colonel.

"Sergeant Durham!" Colonel Tarleton yelled out. "Do you know where Major Poole is? Find him, and inform the major that I need to see him, right away!"

"Yes, Sir!" The sergeant answered. "I believe he was having a meeting with his unit. I will locate him, Sir, and give him your message."

"Good. We have a lot to arrange in the next few hours!" Tarleton exclaimed. He busied himself with plans as he waited for the major to come to his tent. As he was contemplating how to go about his assignment, a knock came on the tent pole. "Enter," he called out.

Major Poole pulled the flap back and walked into the tent. "You needed me, Sir?" He asked.

"Yes, Poole. Some interesting information has come to us that Colonel Marion is going to attack Fort Ninety-Six."

"Attack Fort Ninety-Six? How can he do that with just a few men? Are you sure this is accurate information, Colonel?"

"Yes, quite sure. Sergeant Durham just brought the news. He had been spying on the Swamp Fox and was able to learn this information while in the camp. So, yes, it's a sure thing! Now, we have to make plans to intercept him before he gets to the fort and takes it from the Loyalists who are defending it. General Cornwallis wants you to lead the detachment to take care of the situation. We need to do this immediately, as there is no telling what Marion will do."

"Yes, Colonel," responded the major. "I'll get right on it, Sir! How many men do you think I will need to ambush Marion?"

"Sergeant Durham informed us that Marion's brigade was quite small, maybe only twenty men. So, you shouldn't need a very large detachment. Possibly, a hundred men, no more. You need to be ready to go at dawn, so that you can catch Marion before he gets close enough to the fort to injure it. Make sure you have enough provisions for several days. It may take longer than we expect. Report back to me when you have everything ready."

"Yes, Sir!" Major Poole stepped out of the tent, calling his second-in-command to meet him at his own tent.

Early the next morning, Major Poole and his detachment headed out to cut off Marion's foray into the Fort Ninety-Six area. At the same time, the excited Colonel Tarleton brought his horse under control and called out to his dragoons. He was headed to Marion's headquarters to destroy whatever he could, knowing, unfortunately, that Marion would not be there. Marion would soon be routed by Major Poole's detachment of soldiers. Oh, how Tarleton would love to be there to see that happen! Marion had routed him too many times in the past!

After two days, following Sergeant Durham's questionable directions to the marshland, Tarleton came across one of Marion's campsites. It looked like it may have been Marion's main headquarters, and he treated it thusly. Tearing down tents, destroying papers, and turning his men loose to do whatever they willed, Tarleton smiled at all of the mayhem they were committing. Marion would never use this camp again if Tarleton had anything to do with it! He didn't have the man but he would demolish everything he could in the meantime.

Meanwhile, Major Poole was totally discouraged. He had tried but could not find Marion who was supposedly on his way to Fort Ninety-Six. By now, he was thinking that he had gotten his directions mixed up, or Marion was no longer in the area. Ignorant of the fact that this was just a ruse concocted by Marion, he kept up the search. He was almost two days out from British headquarters and still had seen nothing of Marion's brigade.

Where could he be hiding? he wondered. His scouts had not even found any horse prints that would've proven Marion had been in the area. He knew that within several hours, he would arrive at the fort, and still no Marion. Unless, of course, Marion had already seized the fort and was awaiting the British troops! He plodded on, grasping at the honor he would receive from General Cornwallis if he could defeat Marion and his band.

Much later, Poole and his men arrived at Fort Ninety-Six, only to find that all was calm and nothing was amiss. Marion had not invaded the fort! Everything was as it should be. What a disappointment to Poole that the Swamp Fox had, indeed, outwitted the British again! He realized that Marion had set up a fake battle to confound them. Now, while the British were running around like chickens with their heads cut off, Marion was planning his next escapade somewhere else.

Deciding to let his men rest through the night, Major Poole hastened to speak with the Loyalists holding Fort Ninety-Six. He asked if they had heard Colonel Marion was on his way to drive them from the fort. They had responded that all was quiet and had heard nothing to indicate a coming battle with the rebels. Seemingly, the ruse had been complete. They had been on a wild goose chase!

Heading back to his men, he decided that the best thing to do would be to turn around the next morning and head back to Cornwallis's headquarters, where he would be met with the thunderous voice of his commander.

Tarleton, happy with the day's work of annihilating Marion's headquarters, turned his men's attention to heading back to headquarters. He only hoped that Major Poole had been successful in his own attempt to thwart Marion during this war. Cornwallis should be happy, at least, with Tarleton's part in this, and maybe Poole's part as well. He wouldn't have minded a little skirmish with some of those ragtags that Marion used in his band. But, alas, they were nowhere to be found! So, back to headquarters it was.

After two more days' travel, both Poole and Tarleton ended up arriving at camp at the same time. Cornwallis was eager to hear how things had gone. Had they been successful? Two hours later, the loud voice of General Cornwallis sailed across the encampment. There would be no happiness in the British camp tonight!

Chapter 11

"Riders approaching, Colonel…General," called out the forward patrol. "They are coming at a pretty fast clip, and they don't look too happy, Sir!"

"Is it Thomas and his young friend, Will?" General Marion asked. "I had sent them ahead earlier to scout out the area and make sure there were no British soldiers or Loyalists near the camp."

"Yes, Sir. They are the ones riding their horses at breakneck speed," answered the patrol. "Something important must have happened, Sir! Otherwise, Thomas would not be pushing Ebony at such a fast gallop!" He exclaimed.

As the patrol pulled back to continue scouting the area, Thomas and Will raced up to the general, causing Marion's horse, Ball, to skitter about. "General, General, Sir! We have just returned from checking out your headquarters and it's all in shambles! It was done not too long ago, as far as we could tell," went on Thomas. "We skirted the edges of the area before going in and, Sir, everything was destroyed. It had to have been those galling British dragoons because there is evidence of bayonet thrusts in everything, including your quarters, General."

"Shall we go after them, General Marion?" Will asked.

"No, boys! I am sure that it was that cowardly Banastre Tarleton and his thugs who took advantage of our not being there, which means that our ruse worked and that the spy did his job for us. There was probably no joy in Cornwallis's camp when his detachment returned from a nothing-battle at Fort Ninety-Six. The only thing good for Cornwallis is that Tarleton destroyed my camp, which is just a mere annoyance at this point."

"Fortunately, I always carry important documents and letters with me, just in case something like this happens. So, we won't worry over a few things that we can pick up later. We have other encampments, so we will journey on to one of those. But, before we go there, I do want to see what we can forage from our ruined quarters. Let's move forward, men, and gather what we can from Tarleton's surprise visit. I am just shocked that the sergeant was able to find his way back to our camp, having arrived blindfolded!"

"Buddy!" Marion called. "We will head on to the old headquarters, but I want you to take five men and ride to our camp located on the other side of Snow Island. I am sure that one is still secure because Tarleton was not totally aware of all my other camps, even those built close to this one."

"Yes, Sir, Mr. Marion! By the time you and the men arrive, the camp will have been made ready and food prepared. We will see you soon."

"Thank you, Buddy. Watch out for any Loyalists or soldiers who might be still in the area looking for us. Take care, my old friend."

Worried that General Greene would not be able to contact him further, Marion decided to send a courier, under the protection of darkness, to inform Greene what had transpired in the last few days. But, he would have to do that when he got to his new headquarters. In the meantime, he and the brigade must hurry toward the destruction that awaited them on this side of Snow Island. He was sure that it would not be a pretty sight, and he was right, for when they got there two hours later, it looked like a stormy wind had tossed everything around.

Anything that had been usable was now broken, unimportant papers were lying around on the damp ground, trod upon by horses and men alike, and everything that could be moved was thrown into the fire pit and burned. Shaking his head, Marion, who was usually a positive individual, hunkered down on the ground in dismay. Nothing could be salvaged. Nothing! It had been a wasted trip to come back to his headquarters, which he had dearly loved and grown used to as his home away from his plantation.

But, he knew that his men needed him right now, so up he got, brought his men together, and stoically led them to their horses, stating that there was nothing here that could be reclaimed for future use.

Slowly and wordlessly, his band of men followed him to their horses. They were glad that no horses had been left to the cruelty of the British soldiers. They had been stowed away at a local rebel's farm that was hidden further inland from Snow Island, and they would be retrieved again when Marion needed them.

"Which camp are we headed to?" Major James inquired. "The men are very tired and have not eaten since we broke bread this morning."

"I have sent Buddy ahead to prepare the camp on the other side of Snow Island," responded the commander. "When we get there, the men will be able to relax, enjoy a good meal, and sleep through the night. We all need that, I think," Marion continued. "We will stay at the camp until we hear from either Daniel Morgan or General Greene. But, before I eat, I must prepare a message to send to General Greene by courier to let him know about our last few days."

An hour later, General Marion called Thomas to his tent. "Thomas, I have a letter that must be delivered to General Greene. Since you know his whereabouts, I would like you to do this for me. I want you to have Ebony ready, with your needed provisions, so that you can leave at dawn tomorrow morning. I trust you to deliver this letter as soon as possible, and then return to me with whatever instructions General Greene has for the militia."

"Yes, Sir," responded Thomas. "May I take Will with me?" He asked. "I know that there are British scouts and spies around, so that if one of us gets caught, the other can make his way to Greene's headquarters."

"That's a good idea, Thomas. Inform Will that he will be going with you and that he will need to be ready when you leave in the morning. Thank you, Thomas. Get a good night's sleep as you will need it for your journey on the morrow."

"Will I get the letter from you tomorrow before we leave?"

"No! I have it ready to go. Here it is. Make sure you keep it closely guarded."

"Good night, then, Sir! We hope to be gone and back before you have dinner tomorrow night."

Upon exiting the tent, Thomas spied Will out of the corner of his eye. "Will," he called. "We have a delivery to make tomorrow. Let me tell you about it, as we check on our horses."

"Okay, Thomas," Will said excitedly. Thomas quickly explained the reason for their trek into and through enemy territory.

"We will need to be stealthy because the British are too close to Marion's camps and we don't want to lead them any closer. Are you up to the job?"

"You can count on me," Will answered. "I'll be ready when you are."

"Good," said Thomas. "Get your gear together and then head to bed for a good night's rest. Dawn will be here in a few short hours."

During the night, the hours just seemed to take their time getting to dawn. Thomas and Will both tossed in their bedrolls, with neither young man getting much sleep. The mission upon which they were about to embark could be very important to the war effort. General Greene needed to know what was going on in this part of South Carolina. He had to know where the British were and what they were doing. In order to accomplish this mission, both boys needed to be at the top of their game. Since sleep seemed forever in coming, the boys discussed what they would do if captured by the enemy.

"What shall we do, Thomas, if we are caught with the letter for General Greene? You know that Cornwallis said to hang any rebel that they caught, and Colonel Tarleton gives no quarter. He would hang us all if he could!"

"I know," Thomas answered solemnly. "We just have to make sure that we are not caught. General Marion needs a response to this letter, and he has entrusted us with this assignment, so we have to carry it out, no matter what happens!"

"If it comes to getting caught, we might have to split up and try to confuse the soldiers," said Will.

"Let's just hope that doesn't have to happen," said Thomas. "I think I am tired enough to get some sleep, now. What about you, Will?"

"Yes. I am starting to nod off, and we only have a couple of hours left to rest, so good sleeping, Thomas."

"You, too, Will," said Thomas sleepily.

Chapter 12

The next morning, as the mist was still rising from the surrounding swamp, Thomas and Will were on their way. They had put leather socks over the hooves of their horses to drown out any sound that they would make as they made their way North from Marion's camp. The quiet of the morning seemed to have an unworldly effect on the boys as they rode as silently as ghosts through the swampy wilderness. They stopped, hours later, to have a light lunch, and were on their way again before the sun hit its zenith.

As they neared an area where the British were likely to be, both of them got off their horses and led them through the forest. Indeed, they could actually see the red uniforms of soldiers who had been posted as guards. Quickly, using their hands, they covered the muzzles of their horses so that their whinnying would not attract attention to them.

Ebony, long at the command of his master, seemed to know that he needed to be quiet, although horses could be heard moving around in their corrals. Unfortunately, Will's horse, Saucy, responded to the other horses by letting out a neigh just as the boys sneaked past the patrols.

"Halt! Who goes there?" The sentry called.

Thomas and Will looked at each other and then clambered aboard their horses, regardless of how much noise they were making. They proceeded to gallop away, with the guards calling for help to chase the interlopers.

Before they knew it, bullets were whizzing by their heads, so Thomas and Will rode in a haphazard way to dodge any of the bullets aimed at them. One bullet found its target, though, and creased Will in the arm, but he was able to stay on his horse. "Hurry!" Thomas shouted. "We have to get out of here, now! Those dragoons will be upon us before too long! We need to find a place to hide and take care of your arm."

Several minutes later, it appeared as if they had outrun the British cavalry, and they dared to slow down a little to give the horses a bit of a rest. Ebony and Saucy were pretty well lathered up from the hurried ride. Thomas knew that the horses really needed to stop and cool down. So, looking for a secluded place in the woods, he found a likely spot to rest the horses. As the horses nibbled on the grass, Thomas got his kit from Ebony to take care of Will's arm.

"Come on, Will. Get over here, and let me take a look at your arm. It appears to have bled quite a bit, but it's not really deep, just enough to cause a little blood loss and pain. Let me clean it up and bandage it for you and then we can be on our way again. The horses should be rested enough if we give them a few more minutes. Lie back and let me take care of this arm."

Thomas could tell that Will was in pain but he needed to pour some alcohol over the gash to clean out any debris from Will's shirt that may have gotten in. An infection he did not need. Thomas figured that the doctor at the camp could take a better look at it when they arrived, so he hurriedly dressed the wound as best he could. As he was binding up the wrapping, he could hear hoofbeats in the distance.

"Botheration!" Thomas exclaimed. "Now, what should we do? Getting to General Greene and delivering this letter necessitates our getting away safely! Do you feel able to ride at a good clip, Will? I'm not leaving you behind, so you'd better say that you can get up on that horse of yours!"

"I can make it, Thomas. Just help me to get up and put the reins in my hands. I have ridden under worse conditions than this. Let's go!"

"Alright, then. Let me get the horses. Fortunately, we left the leather stockings on them, so we should be able to move away from the patrol without them hearing us. Okay. Up you go, Will. Hang on tight and we will hopefully be out of this predicament quickly."

The boys could hear the thundering of the horses and the yelling of the soldiers as they relentlessly tracked their quarry. Obviously, they were not worried about being heard by anyone. Now, they could see flashes of red through the trees and knew that they would soon be found. Thomas and Will prayed that they would be able to outrun the soldiers. He knew that Ebony had it in him but he wasn't so sure about Will's mount.

As they neared a clearing, musket shots and yelling startled the young men who were fleeing for their lives. "Oh, no!" Thomas whispered. "They are too close! We will never escape!"

They kept racing until they reached another small clearing, where they were suddenly surrounded by a group of men. Thomas noted that these soldiers were not wearing the red of the British uniforms. These men wore homespun clothing, the same type of clothes that Thomas and Will were wearing.

One man, who appeared to be the leader of the group, came up to their horses and asked, "Who are you and why are those soldiers chasing you?"

Thomas answered, "Aren't the British always trying to chase and catch us American rebels? By the way, thanks for coming to our rescue. I don't think we could have outmaneuvered them much longer. Before I answer your question about who we are, I need to know who you are. Obviously, you are not British soldiers or Loyalists. We would have been swinging from a tree by now if you were."

"That's an easy one to answer," said Bart, the leader of the men. "Those soldiers who were chasing you managed to drive you right into the hands of a few members of Daniel Morgan's militia. General Morgan had us set up this outpost a few miles away from his headquarters in order to thwart any British troops who might carelessly wander too close looking for rebels."

"You do know, don't you, that General Greene has placed General Morgan here in this area to lead and assist with the destruction of British forces trying to take complete control of South Carolina? So, that's why we are here. Now, what's your reason for being in this part of the South?"

Thomas and Will both released sighs of relief. They realized that they had nothing to fear from these men, as they were all on the same side.

Thomas spoke first. "Well, we are on our way to General Greene's camp to deliver a letter from General Marion. While sneaking by those British troops, Will's horse decided to let them know we were in the neighborhood. We ran, they took chase, and now we find ourselves owing you men a great deal of gratitude for stepping in at the right time."

"You mean to tell us that you know this general who has lately come to be known as the 'Swamp Fox'?" Bart asked.

"We do," responded Will, "and we really need to be on our way to get this letter handed over to Greene, so that General Marion will know what his next moves are to be."

"We have found that there is an inordinate number of British troops milling around this area, and we really need a quicker and safer way to get to General Greene. Do you have any ideas?" Thomas questioned. "I know that we must be getting near to the camp but I can't understand why so many British are also closer than they should be."

"That's why we are here," said Bart, the group's leader. "General Greene's camp is still several hours Northwest of here, but there is a way to get around the cavalry. They are staying mainly in the lowlands and staying away from higher elevations, since they know that snipers can hide in the hills. So, my suggestion is that you digress from your route and head toward the foothills of the mountains. That way is more difficult and it might take you a couple of hours longer."

"The only obstacle you might run into is the Scottish Highlanders who are loyal to the Crown. They are a band of fierce warriors commanded by a man named Ferguson. He has led them to some victories against us. They are closer to the North Carolina border, so you might want to stay aware of that possibility. By then, however, you should be near enough to General Greene's headquarters that they won't be a problem for you."

"That sounds like good advice. Thank you. Before we go, though, do you have a man among your group who has some medical knowledge? Will was grazed by a bullet when we were being chased. One of the dragoons got lucky. I did the best I could but I don't want him to get an infection."

"Hey, Watson!" Bart called. "We have a man who needs to have a bullet wound checked. Bring your medical kit and see if you can fix him up."

"Okay, Bart, I'll get my kit and be there in a second." The man named Watson rushed to the campsite to retrieve his pack. "All right, young man. Let me take a look at that arm." As he unwound the bandage that Thomas had applied earlier, he took notice of the amount of blood loss on it. When he got to the wound, it was somewhat red and angry looking, but did not look like any infection was taking place.

He called out to Thomas, saying, "You did a good job on this arm but it needs a few stitches to keep it from festering. Hold on, Will, while I pour some of my special concoction on this wound. It will sting a little but will help heal and numb it as I stitch. Are you good with that?"

"Yes," answered Will. As Watson poured the liniment on his arm, he gasped from the stinging sensation but bit his lips from crying out. A baby, he wasn't!

After Will's arm was tended, Bart offered them some food. Being hungry after running from the British, the boys took them up on the meal. It also gave their horses a bit of a rest as well.

"That horse of yours sure is a beauty," one of the militiamen stated. "Where did you acquire him?"

Thomas explained that his father owned a farm that catered to thoroughbred horses, and that he, himself, had raised Ebony from a foal. "He's my best friend," Thomas said. "I have spent almost more time with him than my own family," he said.

"He appears to have been well-cared for," said Bart. "Now, I suspect you gentlemen want to be on your way. Stay safe and keep your heads down! We may see you again before this war has ended. Give our regards to General Greene."

"Will do, and thank you for your kindness," said Will. "We hope that you stay safe as well."

Chapter 13

Several hours later, having followed the route that Bart had suggested and not encountering any of Ferguson's Highlanders, Thomas and Will could see the outskirts of General Greene's headquarters. They had been fortunate that they had not come across any of their enemies. It had been a long trip and they were happy to have finally arrived at their destination. They had already come across and been stopped by two sets of sentries posted outside of the camp. After explaining who they were and what their mission was, the boys had been allowed to pass. Now they were just outside of the general's tent.

General Greene, upon hearing the arrival of horses, had already stepped out of his tent to see who the newcomers were. Striding up to the boys, he said, "Ah, young Thomas. It's good to see you again. What brings you back to my neck of the woods?"

"It's good to see you in good health, Sir," said Thomas. He then looked at Will and introduced him to the general. "This is my friend, William Francis, Sir. He has ridden with me from General Marion's camp to help deliver this letter to you." Thomas had gotten the letter from his pack while riding into camp and handed it over to the general.

"We had hoped to arrive sooner," he stated, "but we ran into some British sentries who wanted to do us some harm, so they chased us and ended up shooting Will in the arm. If it hadn't been for a group from Daniel Morgan's militia, we might not have made it. They saved us from the British soldiers, took care of Will's arm, fed us, and then directed us to your location. We are in their debt."

"Well! It sounds like you have had quite the trip! Come on into my quarters and let's see what Marion has to say in this letter." As they proceeded to the tent, General Greene called out to one of the soldiers, "Take care of their mounts, Jonesie!" The soldier nodded and grabbed the horses' reins to lead them to the enclosed corral.

"How was General Marion when you last saw him?" He asked. "I admire that man's courage! He can get a lot done with only a few men."

"Yes, Sir, he can. He was fine when we left but he is waiting to see what you want him to do next, aside from harassing the British as he has been doing. His number of men has increased over the time that I have been there. He has about seventy-five men at the camp now, but more than a hundred will show up when he sends out the call."

"Amazing," said the general. "His militia seems to be very loyal to him."

"That we are," said Thomas proudly.

Greene smiled in reply and then perused the letter that Marion had sent. "According to this letter," said the general, "the plan to confuse the enemy about an attack on Fort Ninety-Six caused Cornwallis to send some of his much-needed men to the fort to protect it. He must have been gnashing his teeth when he learned that it had all been for naught. That spy of his fell into the trap without any help from anyone! Marvelous!" He exclaimed.

"What an incredible idea that Marion had. Instead of arresting the man, he used him to further confound the British. That didn't work out well for the spy or Cornwallis, did it?"

"No, it didn't. That spy might receive some words from Cornwallis because of it, and yes, Sir, he is a remarkable man," agreed Thomas. "The only sad thing was the destruction of General Marion's main headquarters while we were away. Marion thinks that it was Tarleton's hatred of him that caused him to just wantonly destroy everything."

"It seemed that Tarleton wanted to inflict as much pain and suffering as he could. Fortunately, all guns and ammunition, horses, and foodstuffs had been relocated before we left this particular camp. Plus, General Marion always takes important paperwork with him so that none of that would fall into the hands of the enemy."

"And wise, too. Let's say we get a bite to eat, men. I'm sure you are wasting away with hunger. Your perilous journey to get here is still not over because you will be returning to Marion's camp tomorrow with new orders for his next mission," Greene stated as they left the tent's enclosure.

After eating a hearty meal of Irish stew and fresh bread, Thomas and Will were led to a tent which they would share for the night. Getting their sleeping gear and packs from their horses, they sauntered slowly back toward their tent to bunk down for a good night's rest. Small hills surrounded their quarters, and the foliage of still-leafy trees created a canopy over them. The peacefulness of the night urged them along as they looked forward to the rest they needed.

Meanwhile, General Greene was in his quarters thinking about future plans for Marion and his militia. It was already early January in the year of 1781 and Greene knew that something had to happen, soon, if the Americans were going to gain their independence. He also knew that Cornwallis, under the direct command of General Henry Clinton, who had returned to his headquarters in New York, had been ordered to get the South completely under British domination.

It seemed that the British were constantly on the march and were eating up territory after territory. As head of the Continental Army in the South, Greene knew he had to inflict more damage on the British Loyalists and Redcoats. However, there was no body of organized Americans left in South Carolina, so he had to rely on those who were part of the militias. He had already enlisted Daniel Morgan and his militia, and with Marion's militia engaged, as well, things could be brought to a head in the South.

Even though Marion's exploits from the swamps and lowlands of South Carolina were certainly hindering British advances in certain areas, more had to be done to keep the British from gaining any further ground. Marion's bold raids with his irregulars often defeated larger bodies of British troops by the surprise and rapidity of their movement over swampy terrain. Greene knew this, and he had already reached out to all of the local militia leaders to gain their cooperation, as well, rather than just issue commands to men who acted independently.

Even Marion still mostly acted independently from what the general expected or commanded. So, right now, he was between a rock and a hard place. What to do was the question.

Early the next morning, after a night of quiet reflection about what needed to be done, a light bulb went off in the general's mind. He had Daniel Morgan close by, and knew just how to use him! He raced around in his tent getting paper and pen to hurriedly send a letter to Morgan. Opening the tent flap, Greene called out, "Thomas and Will! Come here! I have an important message for you to deliver to General Morgan on your way back to Marion's camp. I am sending a message to Marion, as well."

"Yes, Sir," responded the young men, together. "We are all set to go when you have your letters ready."

"If I am not mistaken, you said that you had passed through Morgan's camp on your way here. Isn't that right?"

"We did, General. They directed us to your headquarters. We should have no problem finding General Morgan on our way back."

"Good. Make sure you have everything you need because it might take you a little longer getting back to Marion this time. I have received information that Tarleton and his dragoons are on their way to grab another piece of South Carolina, and I need Morgan to intercept him. Marion is too far out of the way to be of any help this time but I have other plans for him."

"He is a man who is at his best when the odds are most desperate, and right now, we are in that desperate state. I do know that as long as we have free men in South Carolina like General Marion, the war will continue until the enemy is driven from the country."

Within a half hour, Thomas and Will were finished with their packing and were checking in with General Greene. "We're here, General," said Thomas.

"Good. Here are the letters. This one goes to General Morgan and this larger one goes to General Marion. Be careful! The British are still roaming the hills around here. Just last night, one of our patrols came across a small unit of Tarleton's Green Dragoons heading this way. They were sent scurrying off by our soldiers. Just be aware of your surroundings at all times. I wouldn't want you caught with those letters."

"Yes, Sir!" Will exclaimed. "We will be very careful!"

"On your way, then, boys, and a hearty Godspeed!"

Chapter 14

As the boys were delivering their first message to General Morgan, a man by the name of Lieutenant Colonel Henry Lee was being sent to link up with Marion at Snow Island. Greene had previously sent a missive to General Marion telling him of this new addition to his brigade. Marion had been happy with the news and was encouraged that Greene was actually sending him some soldiers from the Continental Army to assist him in their joint offensive operations.

He quickly fired off a letter to Greene, that while he was happy about this, he in no way would give up his leadership of the militia and be under the direction of Lieutenant Colonel Lee.

Also, in answer to Greene's request for more stalwart horses for the cavalry, Marion had responded that there were no 'good' horses to be had because the British had taken all the better horses. Furthermore, his own men needed their horses for the guerrilla tactics they were using to harass the British. They had to have fast-moving horses for their hit-and-run maneuvers. Also, without their mounts, they could not scour the countryside for forage as the general had asked them to do. So, horses were really more crucial to the militia than the regular infantrymen.

Marion was about to send another letter to General Greene explaining, again, his inability to procure more horses for the General's cavalry, when two riders barreled into camp. Thomas and Will had finally returned and Marion was anxious to see what his commander now required of him.

"Well, lads! I had almost given up hope of ever seeing you again. What was the cause of your delay?" Marion asked.

"General Greene had sent us on two missions, one to General Morgan and the second to you. We delivered a message to Daniel Morgan, and he seemed to be quite pleased to receive it. We didn't wait around, though, to see what his orders were, because we knew that the general had also sent a return letter to you," said Thomas.

"We were lucky that we weren't chased by any of Tarleton's dragoons on the trip back. They seemed to be heading in a different direction than we were taking," added Will. "We were curious but were not anxious to get found out again."

"Found out again? What do you mean by that, Will?" Marion asked.

"We came across some Redcoats when we got closer to General Greene's camp and they chased us. If it had not been for General Morgan's outpost of men, close by, we would have been captured. As it was, they saved our necks, and directed us on to General Greene's camp. The British had shot at us, and Will was grazed by a bullet, but his arm has been fixed up now," answered Thomas.

"That sounds like a harrowing experience! I'm glad you made it back to camp safely. So, let me see that letter that General Greene sent. I think you both deserve a nice, long rest after that long ride, so go get some food and then hit your sacks. Have Simon take care of your horses," ordered Marion.

"Yes, Sir. Thank you, Sir!" The boys answered.

"Major James! Peter and Hugh! Come to my quarters, if you would. The general has sent us some orders. Let's see what they entail."

*****

In the meantime, General Morgan was making plans to set General Greene's orders in motion. He had opened the letter and perused it as soon as the two boys had dropped it off. Now, he no longer wondered what General Greene wanted him to do.

Apparently, Greene had received information that Cornwallis was planning to invade North Carolina again, so Greene decided to split his meager army. He wanted Morgan to help him by attacking Cornwallis's rear and flank. So, this was his new mission: attack Cornwallis and force him to change his plans about invading North Carolina. He knew that not only Cornwallis but Tarleton, the scourge of South Carolina, would also be encountered on this mission. With this in mind, he sent a reply to General Greene, expressing his intentions of carrying out his orders.

In his own letter from Greene, General Marion read about the request that was sent to General Daniel Morgan to help delay the British in their plans of invading North Carolina, yet again. He wished General Morgan good luck in this endeavor. As he continued his reading, Greene proposed that Marion should lead an attack on Georgetown, a British-held town on the coast. This was to be done as well as complete the previous tasks given him about procuring as many horses as he could for Greene.

Calling Major James and the Horry brothers to his quarters, he explained to them what General Greene wanted. After discussing the letter, and coming up with a plan of action, Marion called Thomas and Will to him. First, he asked, "Have you boys eaten yet, and have you gotten any rest, along with your horses?"

The boys answered that they had enough time to recuperate their energy.

"Good, because I have some new orders for you two. You seem to work well together and Will's arm seems to be healing nicely, so I have a job for both of you to do. I need you to locate Captain John Postell, whom you met a couple of weeks ago. He has been resting his men at the Goddard Plantation on the Peedee River. Will, you should know where this is since your home is not many miles from there."

"Yes, Sir. I know where the Goddard Plantation is. It should only take us a day to get there."

"Fine," said Marion. "I am not sending a letter with you for the captain as before, in case you are apprehended by the British. Rather, I want both of you boys to memorize what I have to relay to Postell. Can you do that?"

"Yes, General," both boys replied.

"I have always been good at memorizing stuff in school," said Thomas.

"Great! Here is the information I want you to pass on to Captain Postell. Tell him that I have sent several men to reinforce him in this endeavor. In fact, these men will be riding with you. Tell Postell that he needs to collect all the boats and rafts that he can. Then, he is to load them with rice and send the boats to Allston's Plantation. From there, the rice will be ferried to another location to be stored. Also, General Greene wants about fifty Negroes who can be spared from the plantations to serve in the army."

"Will the Negroes be taken from their families by force?" Thomas asked.

"No. Tell the captain that General Marion does not want to distress any family. Only take those who are willing and able to go. Also, boys, I need Postell to give me intelligence of the movements of the enemy in Georgetown, especially their strength in numbers, horses, how many Loyalist militia they have, and if they have any cannon mounted on their protective structures. Colonel Lee is to join me soon, so I need that information about Georgetown as soon as possible. Hopefully, you boys will be back here before Lee arrives. Then, you can join us on this venture."

"This is a lot of information to remember, lads. I hope that you don't forget any points, because they are all important. Do you think you can do it?" Will and Thomas nodded their heads yes, which seemed to satisfy the general. "One other thing that I must ask of Captain Postell is that he needs to deliver to me any men that have taken part with the enemy and I will see that they are punished accordingly."

"We can do this, General," said Will and Thomas together. "We won't let you down, Sir. We know how important any forward action is to the war."

"Get your mounts ready and your gear together. I want you to leave as soon as you are ready, and travel through the night, if necessary. So, make sure you have blankets, water, and enough food to see you through."

"Yes, Sir," they responded.

"Come and see me before you leave," and Marion turned to walk away.

As Will and Thomas hurried to do the general's bidding, a horse galloped into camp.

"General Marion," the rider called. "I have an important dispatch for you from General Greene."

"What now?" Marion muttered. He took the packet from the young rider and then sent him to take care of himself and his horse. He thought that it couldn't be good news, coming so soon after his and Daniel Morgan's letter.

"What does the general want, Sir?" Peter asked. "Are we to meet up with the British and engage them in battle? I hope so. It's about time that we did!"

"Men, General Greene has asked that we make that trip to Georgetown as soon as possible and empty it of any British sympathizers as well as dragoons. He is also desirous of gaining the salt that is produced and stored there. As you know, salt is a scarce commodity right now. With Georgetown being on the coast, that makes it an important transportation hub as well. I am dispatching Will and Thomas, immediately, to Captain Postell to ask him for some intelligence about that area."

"We will leave this encampment as soon as the boys and the other runners get back with further information. In the meantime, as usual, prepare yourselves for a few days' journey away from here. We want to be ready as soon as everyone arrives."

At this point, Will and Thomas arrived back at the general's headquarters, stating that they were ready to leave.

General Marion warned them, "Be careful. There are still Tories around here that would take you to Cornwallis quicker than a mosquito can nip you! I only wish we could get them all on our side. Oh, well, that will happen sooner or later. Be on your way then, lads, and watch out for each other."

"We'll be careful, General," said Will. "We hope to return quickly with a report from Captain Postell."

Thomas and Will made good time and were able to meet up with Captain Postell's brigade early the next day. Fortunately, they hadn't run into any of the enemy this time. They were able to deliver Marion's request, and in return, Postell was able to give them the information that the general needed.

Chapter 15

While Thomas and Will were with Postell, Colonel Lee was finally able to find Marion. After mucking about in the swamp for hours and being lost several times, he had finally come across one of Marion's scouting parties and was guided to the camp. He complained mightily to Marion that he had wasted a lot of time trying to find the elusive 'Swamp Fox'. He asked Marion why he had to conceal himself so far away in swampy territory.

Marion laughed at the question, and answered, "Obviously, it was so that I could not be found, Henry."

Lee scoffed at the answer, saying that he would rather be holed up on a nice plantation than in a swamp full of mosquitoes, snakes, and alligators. Usually a reserved man, Marion actually laughed and then invited Lee into his quarters. He offered Lee a cup of wine which he kept for guests, while he, himself, drank his usual vinegar water. Then they settled down to discuss possible plans regarding the upcoming mission.

Marion told Lee that he had sent two runners to Captain Postell to garner some information on Georgetown, and that he was waiting for them to return before leaving on this operation. He stated that he had also sent out others on errands with some requests to local plantations and backwater areas. He explained the desire of General Greene to take Georgetown away from British control, but Marion wanted to know about the garrison situated there before he arrived. He needed to be aware of what was in store for them. He hoped the boys and the other messengers would be back soon. He was getting antsy.

As he was thinking that very thought, the boys burst into camp with eyes wild with fright. Their horses were all lathered up, declaring that they had to have been galloping hard for quite a distance.

Jumping from their mounts, Thomas and Will both called out at the same time. "General! Dragoons, Sir! Just a few miles from our camp! They must have seen us when we left Captain Postell's quarters."

Taking a huge breath, Thomas explained, "They were on us before we knew it, and if it weren't for the speed of Ebony and Saucy, we would be in their clutches right now! We zigzagged through brush, swamp, and trees, hoping to outmaneuver them. I think we did. We warned the patrol about them, so they are on the lookout," he added.

"Whew! We are glad we made it safely back to you because Captain Postell had some eye-opening news for you about Georgetown," added Will.

"Shall I send my unit out to track them down?" Colonel Lee asked.

"No, I don't think that will be necessary, since we have several guards on the outskirts. They will let us know if the dragoons get too close," responded Marion. "What we need to do, now, is find out what kind of news Postell has for us."

"All right, boys, let's hear the news. Hopefully, it will be helpful to our operations. I'm sure it's stuck in your head somewhere, so bring it out so that we can examine it," chuckled the general.

"Well, Sir, Captain Postell had already scouted out the Georgetown area a few days before we got there, and he already had the information to give to us for you. It seems that there are approximately two hundred British troops garrisoned there, with only one commander and a couple of officers. All seems pretty quiet there with no thoughts that they might be attacked. According to the captain, it will be an easily picked plum!"

"That sounds like very good news, Marion," said Colonel Lee. "We should be able to dispatch that small number of soldiers effortlessly."

"I am familiar with the area around Georgetown," General Marion said. "It is basically where I grew up, and my sister still lives there. I know the streets, the waterways, and the spread of buildings, so let's sit down and come up with a plan that should work."

The two commanders and their aides repeatedly went over the various options as to how the campaign should go. Finally, they came to a decision that was agreed upon by all. Hugh Horry's infantry would use the boats and move down the Pee Dee River and hide on an island near Georgetown. Then, those troops would slip undetected onto the town's waterfront. Peter Horry's mounted men would seize the garrison's commander, while Major James would move into position to cut off the troops from manning the fortifications. Lee's and Marion's horsemen would follow everyone else.

When Marion and the others stepped out of the general's headquarters, Lee was amazed to see not only Marion's original brigade and his own men, but also a much larger group who had arrived while they had been planning. These men were the result of all the errands run by Marion's messengers earlier. Not only were there at least a hundred more men but there was a regatta of rivercraft.

Many of these scows, boats, rafts, and canoes had been commandeered from nearby rivers by Captain Postell, who had received this request from Marion the day before. These rivercraft were all lined up along the swampy river and all the men had to do was step into them!

"Load your infantry in the boats, Hugh, as quickly as possible. We need to move while it is still dark," ordered Marion.

"Yes, Sir! All aboard, men. We have a long hard row ahead of us before the sun rises! Everybody, into the boats!"

Again, Lee was impressed by the militia's speed and was amazed to see how well-oiled Marion's brigade actually was. Within a matter of minutes, all men were where they should be and awaiting the order to proceed.

"Oars in the water, men! Let's move out! Time's a wastin'!" Rhythmically, the men dipped their oars into the water and silently left the shoreline. All that could be heard were the few drops of water landing on the surface as paddles were taken out and put back into the river. It all sounded so natural that nobody would have heard or realized that an army was at the door.

Calling Thomas to his quarters, he told him that he and Will needed to make a second trip to Captain Postell.

"Thomas, I want you to tell the captain that I want him to leave his post as furtively as possible. He is not to tell anyone where he is going. Tell him that I want him to gather all of his men, including those on patrol, and meet Colonel Lee and myself at Kingstree. Tell him not to lose any time but get there as fast as he can."

"Yes, General. We will leave right now," said Thomas.

"Good. Again, be careful! Watch out for Tories, and come back just as quickly as you can because we will be leaving the area shortly to link up with the rest of Lee's militia and those arriving by boat!"

"We'll be back as soon as the message is delivered, Sir."

The plan had been to wait for the men on water to get a good start toward their destination, and then, the following morning, Marion and Lee would follow with their mounted troops, meeting up with Captain Postell and his militia in the designated place, whereupon they would go together to Georgetown.

So, the following morning, the order came to mount up.

"Mount up, men!" Peter Horry ordered. "It's time to be on our way!"

As soon as Horry's mounted men left, Marion and Lee ordered their men to their horses as they would be linking up with Postell and, then, Lee's infantry at Georgetown. Before leaving the encampment, Marion checked to see if Thomas and Will had returned as they would be a part of his own mounted militia. But seeing that they were not yet back from their mission, he decided that they could follow and catch up before too much time had passed. Thinking thusly, he raised his hand and motioned for everyone to head out of camp.

In the meantime, upon delivering the message to the captain, the two young men had jumped back on their horses and headed toward Marion's headquarters, only to find that the General and Lee had already left the campsite. With dismay, they looked around but there was no one or anything to tell them which way to go.

Thomas asked, "Will, what shall we do now? We know that they are heading to Kingstree. Do you know where that is?"

"I do," said Will. "They can't be too far ahead of us. Let's check the fire pit to see if it's still warm." Will walked over and gingerly put his fingers on the coals to see how hot they were. "These are still pretty warm. They've probably only been gone an hour or so. I think that we can catch up in no time. Our horses are fast but they do need a rest. We have done a lot of riding since we left camp yesterday. Let's give them an hour to get their wind back."

"Okay," said Thomas. "I could use a little nap myself. How about you, Will?"

"Sounds like a good plan. If you wake up before me, give me a nudge, and we can be on our way. Let's remove the saddles, so that Ebony and Saucy can have a better rest. It won't take long to resaddle when the time comes," said Will.

The boys rested longer than they thought, and when they both awakened, the sun was getting close to noon. "Wow!" Thomas muttered. "We've overslept! Will, get up." Thomas tapped Will on the leg with his foot and Will slowly stirred. "We slept longer than we should have, Will. Let's hurry and get the horses saddled. We will never catch up to the general at this rate! How could we be such sleepyheads?"

Hurriedly, the boys got the horses ready, grabbed their muskets, and headed out, hoping that the militia had not gotten too far ahead of them. They really wanted to be in this fray with the British.

By this time, General Marion and Colonel Lee had finally arrived at Kingstree, much later than they had anticipated. Their horses had become bogged down in the deep mud caused by recent rains. Marion and Lee had not been happy with the delay but they were there now.

Captain Postell hailed them, saying, "I'm glad you made it, Sir. The roads have been horrendous and our mounts continued to flounder in the muck. We have only just arrived ourselves."

"Good to see you, again, Captain. Are you acquainted with Colonel Lee?" Marion asked.

"Yes, General, we met a while back at a meeting with General Greene. How are you, Colonel?"

"Fine, now that I'm out of all that mire," said Lee.

Chapter 16

"Will," said Thomas. "Where do you think they are? We've been on this road for at least three hours and we still haven't caught up to them. Do you think we took a wrong turn at one of the trails? Do you think they may have taken a different route? I'm getting concerned that we will never reach them before they hasten on to Georgetown. What do you think?"

"Well, if they are plodding through this mud, like we are, then we should be able to catch up pretty soon," answered Will. "If our horses are already tired out from mucking their way through this nastiness, I imagine the general's men are in the same boat," he continued.

"It's getting close to the dinner hour but I doubt the general is going to take time to feed the men before heading on into Georgetown," said Thomas.

"Let's keep moving then. In all this mud, it's hard to see horses' hoofprints, but there are enough indentations to let us know that a herd of horses have come this way already. Let's assume that they are Lee's and Marion's men rather than the British, so just keep your eyes open, Thomas. Hopefully, we should be there soon."

After a few more miles, the road became less muddy and the boys were able to clearly see the hoofprints of horses. These signs were heartening to the boys, making them hopeful of seeing the rest of their militia shortly.

"At last!" Thomas exclaimed. "The end is in sight. If I am not mistaken, that is Simon at the tail end of the line. It looks like he is in charge of the string of horses trailing the forward brigades."

Hearing the sound of hooves behind him, Simon turned around to make sure they were not being followed by dragoons. Recognizing the two young men, he raised his hand in greeting. "Well, you have finally found us! We were all wondering what was keeping you. General Marion didn't want to leave you behind but he needed to keep pace with those who had gone on ahead in the boats. According to him, we are almost at the outskirts of Georgetown."

"Oh, good! We made it in time," said Thomas.

Unbeknownst to General Marion, one of the captains in Colonel Lee's infantry took it upon himself to decide that it was getting too close to dawn, and fearing that Marion would not reach them in time, decided to go ahead with the attack. All they were supposed to do was wait on the island near the Georgetown waterfront and then everyone would attack from their given vantage points. Because the captain did not wait for the go-ahead, Marion's element of surprise was wasted because a sentry at the fortifications noticed the infantry's movement into town and raised the alarm.

"Is that shouting and shots being fired that I hear?" Marion called out. "Didn't those men remember that they weren't supposed to move inland until the word was given?"

Marion and Lee motioned for their cavalry units to gallop headlong into town, but there was not much to see or many to be fired upon as the soldiers who had been awakened had rushed to the stone forts for protection. American bullets were flying but only a few hit their targets. Little damage was done on either side as Marion had his troops pull back as soon as shots began to come from the barricaded forts.

"Let me send my men in and take those barricades," requested Lee.

"No, it would take too many lives and we have no siege equipment with us," stated Marion. "There is no way we can overcome men behind bullet-proof walls that have openings for their guns which can be used against us. It's too dangerous. Our men's lives are more important than that. We will pull back and prepare to fight another day," he said.

As Marion and Lee rounded up their men, infantry and cavalry alike, they began to count how many they had lost. It looked as if only one man had been killed and just two wounded. Marion was always saddened at the loss of any life and he would make sure that this man's family would receive his condolences and praise for a job well done.

"All right, men," he said. "Gather up our wounded and our dead. Let's take care of them and then we will head back to our camp."

As he was speaking, Lt. Colonel Horry came running up to him, and exclaimed, "General Marion! We were able to roust the commander of this town, Lt. Colonel George Campbell, and two of his officers. Our men found him sleeping in his quarters. His officers were found at the tavern. What shall we do with them?"

"Bring them to me, Hugh. I will talk with them," he responded. The men were brought to the general, and after talking to the three men, Marion could not see any good reason for taking them along with him. He released them on parole, stating that if they were caught fighting the Americans again, they would be hung the next time.

The colonel and his two officers agreed to the conditions of parole, and so were allowed to go back to the garrison.

Lee and Marion were disappointed that they were not able to take Georgetown but they knew that there would be another opportunity on another day. The boats were reloaded and the men silently rowed back down the river to Snow Island, while Lee's cavalry and Marion's militia mounted and headed back as well.

Thomas and Will felt keen disappointment that they were unable to take Georgetown, but they believed that it was more reasonable to do as Marion had done—leave the fighting for another day in order to save men's lives on this day.

On arriving back at Snow Island, a letter for General Marion was waiting for him. Noticing the inscription on the letter, it seemed to be an official document. It was entitled 'Letter to Field Commanders: From General Nathanael Greene, Commander of the South Department'. *Good news on this day*, the letter said. Marion looked at the date on which the letter was written: 20 January 1781.

Reading further, he saw that on 17 January, General Daniel Morgan had engaged the British in battle at Hannah's Cowpens. The Continental troops plus local militias had gotten a major victory over the British that resulted in almost total destruction of Tarleton's force. *What good news, indeed*, thought Marion.

Heading out to his team, for he considered them a team working together for the common good, Marion called out. "Colonel Lee, you will want to hear this communication as well. While we were not successful in taking Georgetown, it appears that General Daniel Morgan had a successful campaign against the British at Cowpens. So, it looks like we won't have to worry about Tarleton for a while. Morgan was able to rout him at Cowpens a few days ago and a good share of his men were killed, wounded, or captured."

A loud 'Huzzah' from all the men echoed around the camp.

"Don't get too excited," Marion added. "I am sure that Tarleton will be on the trail, again, looking for us as soon as he gets new recruits. By the way, men, do you remember those two hundred new recruits that we came face to face with a month ago? Well, apparently, they had not yet learned how to fight, and when faced with a counter-bayonet charge by the Continentals, those fusiliers were the first to throw down their guns and fall flat on the ground, begging for mercy! This is all according to Daniel Morgan's report to General Greene. We rebels must have put the fear into their hearts."

The men guffawed at that, knowing that they had taken part in that little skirmish, where those same young recruits had scrambled away, looking for safety behind trees, rocks, and bushes.

Will and Thomas, who had been riding at the tail end of the militia as lookouts, finally arrived in camp, only to hear the men laughing. They wondered at all the chuckling and waited for someone to apprise them of what had occurred. After hearing about Tarleton's routing and the actions of the new recruits, they, too, split their sides laughing after hearing the funny story. Becoming solemn, again, they looked to the general for further words about any future actions.

"General Greene has also informed me that Cornwallis is pursuing Daniel Morgan, burning some of his own supplies in order to move more speedily toward Morgan and his militia. Greene said that he would be linking up with Morgan which should, hopefully, force the British away from their supply lines and leave them in more drastic straits, as far as equipment and supplies go. General Greene has stated in his letter that he will continue the retreat North toward the North Carolina/Virginia border to hold off any further attempts by Cornwallis to take North Carolina."

Marion turned to Colonel Lee, who had been patiently waiting while the general had spoken to all the men. "Colonel Lee, it is with deep regret that I must inform you that General Greene wants you to join his army as soon as possible. So, I must bid you and your men farewell, hoping that we will get to work together again."

"My sympathies, too, General Marion. We get along quite well, and I look forward to being by your side at another time as we fight for our independence here in the colonies." Thus saying, Lee turned to his forces and had them mount up. At the same time, Marion mounted his own horse, and bidding several of his militia to accompany him, they led Colonel Lee and his brigade off Snow Island. Letting his men know he would return shortly, the militia dispensed with preparing to bed down as they were not sure what the orders would be when Marion returned.

In less time than they imagined, Marion was back. He had not finished telling the men what else General Greene wanted from them, so he continued as if he had not been gone for several hours. "The general wants us to keep harassing the Tories in the area as we have been doing. Major James, I want you to go out and raise new recruits anywhere you can. Some of our men have gone home to help their families, and we need to replace them while waiting for those men to return."

"Yes, General," responded James. "I will see how many men I can roust from their comfortable homes!"

Thomas and Will appeared at Marion's right hand, standing at nervous attention. The general looked at them and asked, "What is it, lads?"

Respectfully standing at attention, Thomas uttered, "Sir, may we accompany Major James on his quest for new recruits? We have not helped in this manner before and would like to be of some service."

Marion looked at the two young men, his thoughts scarcely crossing his face. Then, he smiled, and said, "It will be a long, hard ride, boys. Are you rested enough from our Georgetown trip? If you think you can handle it, you are released to go with the major."

"We can handle it, Sir," said Will. "We will go and get our stuff together and be ready when the major leaves," he added happily.

"John, these two will be going with you. Will might be a help, since his home is in the area to which you will be going. Just keep an eye on them, okay, and make sure they don't get into trouble."

"Not a problem, Sir. I will be glad to have them with me. I plan on leaving the majority of my brigade with you, in case you need them for anything, so having Will and Thomas with me will be a big help. We should be ready to leave within the hour."

As the major had indicated, they were all ready to leave in less than an hour. "God go with you," said the general. "We look forward to seeing you back here in a couple of days with a few more men."

Chapter 17

General Cornwallis, now encamped in the Carolina Backcountry, stood with his legs spread apart and his hand on the stirrup of his saddle. Gripping the saddle tightly, he listened without showing any outward emotion as Tarleton recounted the calamity that had occurred at Hannah's Cowpens. As the colonel got to the end of his monologue, the general could not contain his anger a moment longer.

"How on earth could this have happened? We have the world's best soldiers, best-trained, best-equipped, and under the leadership of the best officers. Everything runs smoothly! I cannot fathom such a loss! I grant you that the new recruits were not battle-hardened but there was a sufficient number of men who should have overcome those rebels in no time! What happened, Banastre?"

Again, here stood Banastre under the gun. What could he say, but the truth? "I couldn't tell you, General. All I know is that we had the partisans on the run, and suddenly we were surrounded by Continentals who cut us to pieces and took hundreds of prisoners, my own dragoons included."

Cornwallis looked ready to burst an artery. If his anger against the Americans rose any higher, he might have a stroke, but it was not to be. Words came out of his mouth that Tarleton had never heard the general say before.

"I will chase, find, and destroy that despicable Morgan, if it is the last thing I do! And, we will retake your men, Banastre. We have got to catch and annihilate this Southern army. Destruction of both Greene's Continentals and Morgan's militia will eliminate the threat under which they have us. We have got to get the South under our total domain."

"Morgan humiliated my men and me, Sir," stated Tarleton. "I am willing to offer my resignation if you want it."

"Not necessary, Colonel," said Cornwallis. "You have proven yourself in the past, and one defeat will not destroy my admiration of you as a loyal officer to the Crown. I cannot afford to lose your skill as an officer. I will replace your light corps, lost at Cowpen, with the new reinforcements that just arrived today. We will win this fight, yet!"

After stomping away from Tarleton, Cornwallis, still angry with the Cowpens loss, went to his headquarters to think and plan. He knew that the only way to catch up with Greene and Morgan was to move his army at a faster clip. The Americans carried little baggage and equipment, and so were able to move faster than the British who were encumbered with all kinds of equipment, much being nonessential to the war effort.

Leaving his tent an hour later, he crossed the campground and ordered several sergeants to build a large bonfire. Into this bonfire went everything that would slow his army down or hold it back: personal items, wagons, beds, china, and provisions of any sort. He even got rid of his own personal accessories. His officers and men quickly followed suit. Nothing was left that could be used by the Americans if they should come across his headquarters.

The following day, Cornwallis readied his army and set his men in the direction of Morgan and the British prisoners. Used to having the Tories and Loyalists assist in provisioning his men, Cornwallis discovered that the defeat at Cowpens had disillusioned them, and many feared for their lives, even fleeing their homes. Also, bands of American partisans, intensely devoted to the cause, ranged the countryside, throwing fear into the hearts of those who were not Patriots. Thus, Cornwallis was not able to depend upon them for the foods and animals that they would have readily received from the Loyalists.

Determined to catch Morgan, in spite of his lack of provisions, his troops plodded Northward until they were stopped by a violent thunderstorm that turned the river, over which they must cross, into a turbulent whirlpool. It would be several days before the swollen river would be accessible, so Cornwallis waited it out. Standing on a slight hill overlooking the river, and using his spyglass, he was able to see Morgan's and Greene's army just on the other side. Oh, how he wanted to get across that river!

He called out to Tarleton, "Here's our quarry, just waiting for us, Colonel. All we have to do is cross this water."

Crossing the water did not turn out to be a good idea, as General Cornwallis's men were either fired upon by the militia, or drowned in the swirling water. While many survived the crossing, this skirmish cost the British too much in men, horses, and equipment. However, Cornwallis was still determined to win this war! *My day will come*, he thought.

Chapter 18

With Lee joining Greene's forces after their unsuccessful trip to Georgetown, Marion found himself alone, again, with just his men to protect each other, and continue the harassment of the Tories in the area. Oh, well. This was the way it had been throughout the whole war. He and his men would endeavor to follow through on General Greene's orders.

It was now March of 1781, over a full month since Georgetown, and many of Marion's men had not yet returned from visiting their families. He was still waiting for Major James to come back with the promised recruits. Nothing was happening at this point and Marion was starting to get antsy again. He was not one to sit still when there was work to be done to save this new country of theirs. However, he was not the one in control, so he sat, waiting for further orders from General Greene.

"A messenger coming in, Sir," yelled Simon. "It looks like another dispatch from General Greene."

Marion hurried out of his quarters. "It's about time," he said. As he was handed the letter, he noticed that the handwriting was not Greene's at all, but a missive from General Sumter. Of all the generals, this was from an unexpected source, since Sumter had turned up his nose at Marion and his militia the year before.

Marion read the letter and immediately called out to Peter Horry. "General Sumter is attacking the British depot at Fort Granby and he wants us to keep the British General Rawdon away from him. He is trying to get hold of all the supplies at that fort for another campaign."

"It's not a very good idea in my opinion," Marion said. "The British have been reinforcing all their forts in this area and Sumter doesn't have enough men in his regiment to take any of the forts."

"What are you going to do, General?" Peter asked.

"He is my superior, so I guess we have to do as he asks. Round up as many men as you can while we await Major James. Hopefully, he will arrive soon. I need to send Thomas and Will on another mission, so keep an eye out for them, as well."

"Will do, General. I am on my way," said Horry. "I shall return as soon as possible."

In the meantime, Sumter had to withdraw from Fort Granby and decided to attack Fort Watson, which was well-defended by the British forces. After losing several men, Sumter had to call off the attack, again, and hustle what was left of his regiment to a plantation nearby. From here, he sent another message to General Marion.

The following day, after having sent Peter Horry out to round up more of his militia, Major James returned with about a hundred men who were ready to do battle. Peter Horry returned, also, and said that many men were not enthusiastic about this foray, and so would not answer the call of the Swamp Fox this time.

On top of that, unbeknownst to Marion, Rawdon had taken command of the British forces in South Carolina, and was now planning his own attack on Marion's Snow Island base. Unfortunately for Rawdon, however, there were some unknown Whigs close by who were posing as turncoats to the cause. These Whigs silently sent a message to Marion about Rawdon's plans.

Getting that particular bit of information from the two Patriots caused Marion to jump into defense tactics. Receiving and appreciating the advice of Major James and the Horry brothers, Marion called his now much larger group of men together.

"Fellows," he said. "We have just been warned that Colonel Rawdon, the man Cornwallis has put in command of the British forces in this area, is planning a strike against us here, on Snow Island. We must stay vigilant! I am sending Will and Thomas to scout out the area and alert us if and when they see any British soldiers. In the meantime, I will be making ready the main force of men which I will take with me to lay a trap for the British before they suspect anything is amiss."

"Thomas and Will," he called. "I want you to ride at least 10 miles out of the camp and keep your eyes open for the enemy, whether it be dragoons, fusiliers, Tories, or Loyalists. Report to me if you see anything at all!"

"Yes, General," said the boys, as they hurried to their horses. They were so excited to be sent on this errand as part of the general's defense plan.

Jumping on to their mounts, the two young militiamen waved to the general as they took off down the trail leading away from the camp.

It didn't take the boys long to reach their 10-mile limit. Scanning the horizon, they could not see any color of uniform, whatsoever. They assumed no one was around and were about to return to camp, when several British soldiers, who were hiding in the brush, jumped out at them. They didn't have enough time to pull their muskets from the scabbards on their saddles.

"You, there! Get off those horses, and do it now," a soldier yelled. With a hard-eyed glint he continued, "Unless you want to feel a bullet in your hearts, keep your hands away from your muskets."

Slowly getting off their mounts, Thomas said, "No need to get hasty, boys. We're not here to do anyone harm. We are just two boys out enjoying an afternoon ride. Actually, some of you may know Will's father, who is a fierce Loyalist and owns the Francis Plantation not far from here."

"I know the Francis Plantation," piped up another soldier, "and I have met Mr. Francis. He definitely is a Tory! This guy, Will, is his son, because I have seen him at General Cornwallis's headquarters when his father was visiting. You are quite a ways from home, Will. What are you doing out here by the swamps?"

"Actually," Will said, "we were hoping to catch sight of the Swamp Fox. We have heard so much about him and how he has consistently been harassing us. We were told that his headquarters are somewhere around here, and we were just checking out the area. By the way, what are you men doing out here, so far from your own company?"

George, the soldier who had spoken to them first, said, "We are an advance guard of Colonel Rawdon's army and were sent to basically spy out the region just as you are doing. We hope to not just see the Swamp Fox but to actually catch him! What a feather that would be in our caps!"

Will and Thomas looked at each other. Here was the information for which General Marion was looking. Now, how to get away and report this to their commander?

"So, men, are you planning on capturing us as the enemy, or are you going to let us, who are British Loyalists, go?" Thomas asked.

"Well, since we know that Will is a Loyalist, we figure that you are on the same side," said the corporal. "I don't see any reason to detain you, since we are all looking for the same person."

"Thank you, Corporal," responded Will. "If we see the Swamp Fox, we'll let you know. Good hunting, men!"

The two boys mounted their horses, again, and turned to wave goodbye to the soldiers, who saluted them in return.

Cantering at a leisurely pace so as to not cause any suspicion, Thomas looked at Will and snickered. "Whew! That was close," he said. "Good thinking on your part, Will, pretending we were Loyalists looking for the Swamp Fox," he added.

"I can't believe we got away with it," replied Will. "Now, we'd better hurry to catch the general before he leaves camp. We need to let him know that this way out is not safe. No telling how many soldiers were hiding back there, waiting to spring out on him, like they did with us."

Patting Ebony, Thomas responded, "Let's get out of here fast, then. I think we have left the British far enough behind that they won't see which way we're going." So saying, he slapped his reins causing Ebony to move forward at a quicker pace. Will followed suit and they sped up to a gallop, riding side by side when possible.

Nearing the camp and the lookouts, Thomas called out the password, and then exclaimed, "The British are closer than we thought. We need to let the general know!"

Having received permission to pass, the boys galloped into camp. Seeing that Marion was just getting on his horse, the boys rushed over to him and informed him about the British soldiers who were not too many miles away.

Turning to his men, Marion said, "Okay, boys. We have to change our plans slightly. We will not use the normal exit from the swamp but use the hidden passageway that will take us around them. Then we will continue on our mission to waylay those British soldiers." Before riding away from the boys to lead his men, Marion turned to them and said, "Good work, men! You have done well. I am proud of you both. Now get in line with the rest of the militia," he commanded.

Thomas looked at Will. "That's the first time he's called us 'men'," he whispered.

"You're right," responded Will. "Let's get over there, so that he doesn't have to refer to us as boys again."

Moving along at a good clip, General Marion led his army toward the location of Wyboo Swamp, where he planned to lay an ambush for the British.

The colonel in charge of the British troops had been informed that a causeway passage there would be the best spot for Marion to lie in wait to ambush him. Knowing this, the British Colonel Watson did not cross the causeway, but instead, sat upon his horse staring across the passageway at Marion and his men who had just arrived, and who were now staring right back.

As Marion looked across the way, he could see the wonderfully-uniformed troops of the world's greatest army. Then, turning his head and looking around at his own poorly-equipped militia who sat quietly waiting for orders, he considered that he was glad he had Major James and the Horry brothers on his side, even if they were all dressed in homespun. He knew that this battle would be important for his men because today would be an open battle, not a hit-and-run raid, or guerilla ambush.

He had not gained the advantage that he had hoped for, so he retreated to the woods with most of his men and set Peter Horry and his cavalry at the front by the swamp. Since Thomas and Will had their own mounts, they became a part of Peter's group of horsemen.

Thomas and Will stayed close together and watched each other's backs during the back-and-forth series of charges and countercharges from both sides. Since they were situated at the back of the cavalry, they did not receive the brunt of the battles but they made ample use of their guns and swords during the fray.

Again, General Marion seemed a step ahead of the British because every bridge over the river they tried to cross had already been demolished by Marion's men, who had been sent ahead earlier to destroy any structures built over those waters. American marksmen then frustrated the colonel's attempts to cross each bridge, so that he had to take refuge at a nearby plantation where he hoped to be reinforced by more troops.

Once more, the British had been routed by the American Patriots! While Watson had taken refuge at that nearby plantation, Marion gave his men leave to rest themselves and their horses while they awaited Watson's next move. They didn't have to wait long. In fact, Marion was surprised one morning when a rider was seen coming from the plantation and he was holding a white flag.

"Rider coming," called out Will, who was on patrol that particular morning. "He's carrying a white flag, Sir." Excitedly, he asked, "Do you think Watson is going to surrender himself and his troops?"

With a frightened look on his face, the rider, a young private, galloped into camp and asked to speak with General Marion. Coming toward the soldier, Marion held up his hand and asked what he wanted.

"With respect, Sir, Colonel Watson wants to know if you would be so kind as to allow his wounded soldiers to leave the plantation and ride to Charleston for medical help."

Marion responded in a friendly manner. "I will allow all wounded men to leave but without their guns and ammunition."

"Yes, Sir! I will tell the colonel that, and thank you in advance for allowing those men to leave. We are in your debt." Without any more words said, the young man turned his horse and quickly took off for the plantation, just in case Marion changed his mind and decided to capture him.

"Will! Thomas! Follow that young soldier and see that my orders about no guns or ammunition are carried out," ordered Marion. "Stay well behind him, so that he doesn't know he's being followed."

"Yes, Sir," the boys replied. Thomas and Will headed to their horses. Since their mounts were already saddled in preparation for anything that the general might need, they didn't have to waste time saddling them.

"Be careful, men. Don't let yourselves be captured," Marion commanded as they rode away.

"We will, Sir," answered Thomas. "We will make sure that everything is carried out according to your orders."

They took off in a hurry, for the British soldier was making haste to get back to Colonel Watson to let him know what Marion had said.

"Thomas, hold up," said Will. "We don't want him to be aware of us, so we need to use caution. Let's go slowly and stay as far behind as necessary, but be able to keep him in our sights."

"Okay, Will. Ebony is wanting the exercise but I'll hold him back. When we get closer to the plantation, we can scout out some trees to hide behind to make sure that no weapons or ammunition are loaded onto the wagons carrying the injured soldiers."

"Hey, there they are! The wagons are already being pulled up to the house and the injured are being placed in the back. Watson must have thought that Marion, a caring man, would say 'yes' to his request, and ordered the wagons around earlier. I don't see any weapons being slid in, do you?" Will asked. "Maybe they are actually going to do only what was ordered by the general.

Let's wait until they roll out before we head back to camp. I want to make sure that everything is on the up-and-up!"

After waiting for another half hour, it seemed as if all the wounded soldiers had been laid in the wagons. Will and Thomas counted about fifteen wounded and would report that number to Marion. As the wagons turned away and headed down the long drive toward medical care, the boys turned their horses and headed back to camp.

Chapter 19

About a half hour later, while the boys were on their way back to camp, Thomas sidled Ebony up close to Will's Saucy and whispered, "Did you hear that? It sounded like gunfire! Should we check it out?"

"I think you're right! I heard it, too," responded Will. "Let's see what's going on."

Immediately, they both turned their horses to the right and headed in the direction of the gunshots. Getting closer, the two young men saw three Patriots running full out, with several dragoons chasing close behind. The three men were afoot and would be caught soon if no one helped them.

"We've got to do something!" Will said. "Those guys are going to be captured or shot in the next few minutes."

"I've got an idea," Thomas said. "Just follow my lead. Take your feather out of your hat and turn it around. It will make us look more like the British civilians around here. Ho, there, fellow Loyalists!" Thomas called out. "Who or what are you shooting at? The Swamp Fox?" He chuckled. "We've been on an errand for Colonel Watson, scoping out the area around the swamps. He is in a big hurry to add the elusive General Marion to his list of accomplishments before he heads back to General Cornwallis."

"We were chasing three of those homespun Patriots. They were getting too close to our camp and our captain ordered us to follow them and see where they went, actually, in hopes of finding Marion," one of the dragoons said. "Now, you have held us up and they've gotten away. Thanks a lot, friends!" He said sullenly.

"Well, we can help you look for them if you want, but they are close enough to the swamp to be well-hidden by now. We are sorry you lost them. They were probably running toward their camp."

"No matter," said the leading corporal. "We will just tell our captain that we chased them a long way and that they won't be coming back. Thanks for your offer, anyway. Hope you find that wily Swamp Fox! We will be heading back to camp now. Mount up, boys, let's be on our way!" He ordered. With a wave of his hand, the corporal led his squad back the way they had come.

"Whew," said Will. "That was a close one! Let's find those three men and see who they are and what they are up to. Someone may have been wounded during the chase. We'd better put our caps on right and put the feathers back in. We don't want to get picked off by our own militia."

Riding further down the trail, they were soon hailed by the three men they had helped get away from the British.

"Ho, there, fellows," said the oldest man of the group. "We are so glad you happened along. You saved our hides! Thanks, so much. We were on our way to sign on with General Marion when those soldiers spied us. We hadn't expected to find any British so close to Marion's camp."

"So, where do you come from?" Thomas asked.

"We're part of the local militia and decided that we would rather be a part of General Marion's men. He seems to know more about what is going on in this area than our local leader. We have no horses, so we were hoping that he would outfit us. We only have our muskets."

As the two boys were very knowledgeable about the area and surrounding militias, Will decided to find out if these men were actually telling the truth. Will began to question them further about their militia, its commander, and where they were headquartered. After all, it could just be a ploy to get Thomas and Will to lead them to Marion. If they were too hesitant about answering the questions, then they could be British soldiers dressed as Patriots, just scouting for someone to lead them to General Marion's headquarters to do who knew what.

After questioning the men further, Thomas and Will looked at each other. They both knew that these men were not who they said they were. Their hesitance in responding to the questions showed that they could have picked up bits and pieces of information along the way, just enough to sound like they knew what they were talking about. Their uncertainty was a clincher for the boys.

Moving further from the men, Will and Thomas whispered between themselves. "These guys are not who they claim to be," said Will, lowering his voice.

"I agree," responded Thomas. "They aren't any militiamen from around here. What shall we do?"

"I suggest that we pretend that we believe them and take them on into camp, and let General Marion take care of them," said Will.

"Okay," said Thomas.

"All right, men. It seems that you are who you say you are, so we will guide you into camp but you need to be blindfolded first."

"Sounds good to us," the leader said. "Lead the way. You can even use our scarves to blindfold us."

"We have a way to go," said Will, "so we won't blindfold you yet." Both boys got off their horses and started walking with the men between them, Will at the front and Thomas at the rear. After adding blindfolds sometime later, and walking the men for over an hour in a roundabout way, Thomas pursed his lips and gave the password to the guard on duty. Unbeknownst to the three men, this password indicated enemies would be coming into camp. Knowing this, the guard passed the information along to the next lookout.

Thirty minutes later, the three men found their blindfolds removed abruptly and had their first sighting of General Marion and his camp. Expecting to see everyone sitting lazily around, the men were surprised to find General Marion atop his horse, with his gun in hand, pointing it at the three men. He was surrounded by his cavalry, who also were pointing their rifles at the men. Too startled to speak, the newcomers looked around at the hostile company.

Marion pointed at the men, and in a beguilingly soft voice, asked, "Who are you and what are you trying to find out?"

"Well, General, as we told these lads here, we want to join up with your militia. Nothing else is on our minds, Sir!"

"For your information, men, these two 'lads' here are experienced fighters and are most knowledgeable about what is going on in this area. They figured out right away that you are not part of any militia in this region or even Patriots for that matter, but British Loyalists or soldiers engaged in learning more about this camp and our plans. Therefore, sirs, you are spies! Shackle them, men, and tie them securely to that large tree in the swamp. Hopefully, the alligators will leave them alone."

"Oh, no, General!" They sputtered. "We are not spies, as such. We were just told by our commander to get into your camp somehow and look around at what you had and hear your plans, if you had any. Also, we were to acquire any information on General Greene. Please! Have mercy on us!"

"What you have just said has sealed your fate because spying is what you are doing. Tie them up quickly! We have things to do. By the way, who is your commander?" Marion asked.

"General Cornwallis, Sir. He's the one who sent us to do this. He is still mad about his men under Tarleton losing at Cowpens. He is determined to finish off your militia."

"Well, we'll see about that!" Marion said. He then turned to Thomas and Will, and asked, "Did you men see that all went well with Colonel Watson's request, and that they did only what they were asked to do? You saw no arms or ammunition on the wagons, just wounded soldiers?"

"Yes, Sir," responded both of them at the same time.

"Okay, then, men. We have other orders that must be carried out, so let's mount up and be on our way."

"Wait!" The leader of the spies called. "What about us? You can't leave us tied up like this, especially with alligators staring at us!"

"It's that, or be hanged. Which would you prefer? Unless, of course, you have other information that would be pertinent to us," said the general.

The spies looked at each other, wondering if they should offer any more information that might get them off the hook and save their lives. Would it be worth it, especially if Cornwallis found out that they had tattled on his plan?

"If you have anything to say, then, out with it! My time is too valuable to be wasting it on you. Speak up!"

"All right," said the leader. "Here's what we know. General Greene has a spy within his camp and we were sent here to find out if Greene has discovered him, yet."

"And why would I know something like that?" Marion asked.

"Well, Sir, everyone knows that you and General Greene are close. Therefore, if anything like that occurred, you would have been informed by the general, himself," said the spy. "Since General Cornwallis has not received any reports back from his informant, he has assumed that the spy has been imprisoned or possibly executed."

"Do you know who this spy is?" Marion asked.

"No, Sir, not by name, but I would recognize him if I saw his face," said Rufus, the one in charge of the three. "One more thing, General, Colonel Doyle is on his way to Snow Island to find this camp and destroy it."

"Thomas! Will! You both know where General Greene's camp is. He is on his way to North Carolina and I need you to find him fast, and let him know that he has a spy in his midst. Take Rufus, if that's his real name, with you. He can recognize the spy. If he tries to get away, shoot him. These other two will be left tied up outside of camp and you can free them after you have alerted General Greene."

"Yes, Sir," both young men responded as they climbed back up on their horses.

"Simon, ready horses for these three spies," commanded Marion. "One will go with Thomas and Will, and the other two will ride with us until we get off Snow Island," he said.

"Any particular horses, Sir?" Simon asked.

"Don't we have a couple of old plodders in the pasture?" Marion asked.

"They should do for these two. Give Rufus a faster horse because Will and Thomas will be in a hurry to reach General Greene."

"Getting it done, Sir. We should all be ready to go in a matter of minutes."

"Untie these men and put them up on the horses as soon as possible," ordered General Marion. "We need to move out of camp soon."

The three spies looked relieved that they were not to be left as the next meal for the alligators, but they knew that their necks could be in a noose if the spy in Greene's camp was not found. They soon found themselves blindfolded again, and knew that there was no way they would be able to find their way back to this camp. Their only hope of escape would be if Colonel Doyle found them and the camp before they could be hanged.

Chapter 20

Thomas and Will led Rufus's horse, Barney, down the trail away from the camp and headed Northeast in search of General Greene's headquarters. They plodded on quietly, watching out for any Redcoats who might be lurking in the tall grasses and cattails near the swamp. After an hour, they took Rufus's blindfold off him but kept their hands on his reins.

Starting up a conversation, Thomas asked, "Rufus, why do you think that you will recognize this spy in General Greene's regiment? Do you know him at all?"

"I don't know his name but he used to come calling at my sister's door before the war started. She didn't like him, so he stopped calling after a while. I guess he finally got the hint," Rufus said. "I didn't like his ways, so I was happy she didn't encourage him further."

"Does he have any physical traits by which we could recognize him?" Will asked. "A limp, red hair, scars, blue eyes, or anything else that would give us a clear idea of what he looks like?"

Rufus thought for a moment, then his eyes lightened up. "Yeah! He has a big red birthmark on his left cheek that's shaped like a seven. He could disguise himself but he couldn't get rid of that!"

"Okay, that's something we can look for," said Thomas.

The three of them continued on, keeping an eye out, the boys watching for the enemy, and Rufus watching for anyone who could rescue him. After galloping a good distance, Thomas and Will stopped at the bottom of a hill. This was the spot where they had gotten help from Colonel Morgan a short time ago. But, alas, he wasn't here today. They realized, then, that he was on his way to assist General Greene and his campaign to rout General Cornwallis in North Carolina.

"Why are we stopping here?" Rufus asked.

"Oh, just remembering how we were here not that long ago, when Will, here, was shot in the arm by your comrades. We received help in this area."

"From whom?" Rufus asked.

"Can't say," said Thomas. "That's confidential information!"

"Well, let's get a move on," said Will. "We still have a while before we get to General Greene's camp, if we can find him."

After two more hours of steady riding, the boys were stopped by a loud command. "Ho! Who goes there?" A raspy voice asked.

"Thomas Sinclair and Will Francis are here to see General Greene on urgent business that requires immediate attention. Please let him know we are here. He knows us!" Thomas called out.

"Wait right there while I check you out," ordered the guard. The boys heard the guard send the message down the line to all the lookouts. Finally, after waiting several minutes, the word came back to send them in. "All right," said the guard. "You have been cleared to enter."

Making their way along the trail as quickly as they could, Thomas and Will spotted General Greene talking to one of his majors. He looked up when he heard the horses entering the compound and waved at the boys.

"What urgent news do you boys bring me today?" He asked. "I see that you have brought a stranger into camp with you. Does he have something to do with what you have to tell me?"

Will spoke first. "This is a British spy, General, who tried to infiltrate General Marion's camp, along with two others. General Marion found them out and discovered why they were spying. That's why we are here to see you. This spy, Rufus, told us that General Cornwallis has inserted a spy into your regiment and he is here in this camp as we speak."

The general looked flabbergasted. He knew that there were spies all over, but none in his camp, he thought. "So, why is this spy with you, boys?"

"Well, General, Rufus here knows what your spy looks like and can identify him for you," commented Thomas. "Since none of us know his name, this is the only way General Marion figured we could catch him. We do know that he has a red birthmark on his left cheek. That should help us recognize him."

General Greene muttered, "A spy in the camp. A red birthmark."

Suddenly, his wide eyes became slits as he realized that he knew this spy! "Major Nelson," he called. "Send for Corporal Grey! I want him in my tent immediately!"

"Yes, General," he replied.

Within five minutes, Corporal Grey was standing in front of General Greene, and his commander's face did not look happy. As he looked around the tent, his eyes rested on Rufus, and his complexion suddenly paled, making the red scar on his face stand out all the more.

"What do you have to say for yourself, Corporal, or should I say British spy?" The general asked.

"British spy, Sir? I…I…I don't know what you…you…you mean," the corporal stammered.

"Do you recognize this man sitting here?" Greene asked.

"N…No, S…S…ir," he continued to stammer. "I've never seen him before in my life!"

"Come now, Corporal. This man, Rufus, said that you used to court his sister, or tried to. Are you denying that?"

"Yes, General. Please, Sir, I am a loyal Patriot. I don't know anything about being a spy!"

"Major Nelson! Has this man been out of camp in the past four weeks?"

"Yes, he has. One night about two weeks ago, he pawned off his guard duty to another soldier, saying that he had an urgent message to carry somewhere. Last night, he was seen sneaking away but was brought back before he could go anywhere. He has been on kitchen patrol duty this whole day as punishment. Why do you ask?"

"Apparently, our young corporal here is a British spy, and has just been recognized as such."

"What kind of soldier has he been, Major?"

"Well, Sir, as far as I know, he has followed orders and gone into battle with us like all the rest. However, I have noticed that he never really fires at anyone, or if he does, he always misses. I just considered him a poor shot."

Turning back to Corporal Grey, who was now shaking, the general asked, "Do you want to save a noose around your neck and tell us who you really are? You know the punishment for being caught as a spy! I am willing to give you a choice. Either tell us what you are doing here and become a prisoner until the end of the war, or receive the death penalty."

Corporal Grey decided that he had truly been found out. He didn't know how he was going to get out of this situation. He had spied several times for General Cornwallis and had never been discovered, so this was quite a blow to him. But he had to give an answer and give it quickly if he wanted to survive. The truth was the only thing that would save him now, so the truth came out. "I was sent by General Cornwallis, my commander. He had ordered me to find out how many soldiers you had quartered here with you and what your future plans were for North and South Carolina."

"And have you given him that information, Grey?" General Greene demanded.

"Yes, Sir. The last time I was out of camp, I met a courier that was waiting for me and sent whatever information I had back to General Cornwallis."

"And what information was that, Corporal?" The general asked.

"Three full regiments, Sir," responded Corporal Grey.

"W…wh…a…a…t?" General Greene sputtered. "Can you not count, Corporal? There is no more than a regiment and a half at this location! Why did you give him such an outlandish number?"

This time, the corporal's face turned bright red, so red that it almost eliminated the birthmark on his face. "Er…um…" he stammered. "I really want to change sides, General, and I thought if he knew you had such a large number of troops, he would not attack this post. I haven't given him any other information, Sir, because I didn't have any to give. That's it, Sir! I have seen how determined the Americans are about defending their rights, and I agree with them. I just want to be on the right side. I had to give General Cornwallis some information, or he would have become suspicious."

Calling to the sergeant standing outside of his quarters, the general called him in, and pointing to the corporal, ordered, "Take him to the guardhouse until I can decide what to do with him!"

"Yes, General," the sergeant said as he grabbed the corporal by the arm.

"No, please! I am telling the truth, General Greene. Please don't hang me! I really want to become a true Continental soldier."

"Take him away, Sergeant!"

After the men were out of sight and out of hearing, Greene leaned toward Major Nelson. "What do you think, Major? Is he being on the up-and-up about joining the Continental Army, or just trying to save his neck? I don't know the boy at all, and maybe he did give counterfeit information to Cornwallis. Apparently, he has been here long enough to garner enough facts to pass on to the enemy, although he said that he has only given misinformation, but I don't think I can trust him fully, yet," the general stated.

"How about giving him some more false facts to deliver to Cornwallis?" The major asked.

"We can't be sure that he would carry out that last bit of information. He could just as easily stay with General Cornwallis and tell him that he had been found out. Of course, Cornwallis might just wonder how the corporal got out of the guardhouse to bring another message. That would certainly be suspicious to me. He would know, then, that the corporal was delivering wrong communication. No," continued Greene, "I think that we are better off keeping him here under close observation."

"Let's induct him into the Continental Army as a private, and give him a soldier, whom we know to be very loyal to the cause, to be his constant companion. Maybe he will prove to us that he really does want to join us. What do you say, Major?"

Major Nelson nodded his head in agreement. "I think that might be the best solution, Sir. I will speak to one of my sergeants to see which private we could place with Grey."

"Okay, then. I will leave the rest of this in your hands, Major," concluded Greene.

"Thank you, Sir. We will figure out which side this Corporal Grey is really on," responded Major Nelson as he left the general's quarters.

It was apparent that General Greene had forgotten that Thomas, Will, and Rufus were still in his quarters because he was slightly startled when he turned around and found them still there. "Oh, boys," he said. "I totally forgot that you were the ones that brought this spy incident to me. I appreciate your loyalty to the cause, Thomas and Will. The question, now, is to decide what to do with this Mr. Rufus here. Since he has been helpful in this case, I think that we can take the death penalty off the table."

Rufus, who had been silent through all of this, breathed a sigh of relief.

General Greene continued as if thinking out loud. "We can't send him back to Cornwallis, and General Marion doesn't need him slowing him down, so I guess that we will just have to confine him until the end of the war."

Thomas sidled up to the general and whispered in his ear. "Sir, Rufus is not a British soldier but an American who sided with the British. Do you suppose that we could convince him to join us, instead of spending the rest of the war in the stockade?"

"And how would we determine that he would remain loyal to us, Thomas?" The general asked.

Motioning to Will to join him and the general, Thomas suggested, "You could offer him amnesty based on two or three conditions, Sir."

The general pulled the two young men further into the corner of the room, and asked, "To what conditions would you think Rufus might agree? I have my own ideas. I just want to know what your suggestions might be."

"Well, first off," said Will. "I would have him sign a document stating that if he joined us and then decided to go back to the enemy to work as their spy again, he would forfeit his life when recaptured."

Greene nodded and said, "Those were my initial thoughts, so I agree with that proposal, Will. I think that he needs to also promise that he will serve as a loyal soldier, doing what he can to help us get rid of the Redcoats. Further, until he has proven himself, he will need to be in the sight of someone at all times, even when he is sleeping."

"Those conditions sound good to me, General. If I were in his place, I would grab at the chance to live a full life, rather than waste away in a prison somewhere," said Thomas.

"Let's talk to Rufus and see what that chap has to say, shall we?" Greene asked.

Turning toward the pale-faced Rufus, the men strode toward him. "Well, Rufus, have you had enough time to decide what punishment would be appropriate for you?" The general questioned.

Rufus gulped noisily. He did not know what the outcome of that discussion was but he knew in a flash that they had been talking about him. "Well, General, could I possibly join the Continental Army? I have not been trained as a soldier but I can shoot really well. I think that you could even use me to spy on the British because I really am getting tired of seeing what they are doing to our country."

"I only agreed to help them in order to protect my family. If I hadn't helped them, they would have put my parents and siblings out of their home."

"I can't really trust you at this point, Rufus, but I am a man who will give second chances if the person asking is sincere, and I believe that you are genuine in your request. However, having you sent back as a spy would only put you into more jeopardy because, by this time, the British know that you have been detained by us. So, this is my plan. You will sign a statement saying that you have become a true and loyal Patriot to the cause, and you will become a part of my detail here, where you will be under constant supervision. If you agree to these conditions, we will see about granting you amnesty."

"Oh, thank you, General! I will be forever in your debt if you allow me to do that. I'll sign a statement right now! I don't even have to think about it! And you will be able to trust me fully in the future," responded Rufus.

"Very well, then, Rufus. As soon as you sign your pledge, consider yourself a part of the Continental Army and be treated as such from now on. It may take a little while for all of the men to trust you, since they know you as only a spy for the British, but they will come around as you share meals, sleeping quarters, and workload with them."

"Thomas and Will, it appears that your trip here is at a conclusion. Thank you for bringing Rufus to my attention. I think that we can handle him from here. So, I am releasing you to head back to General Marion with my thanks. Make sure you stop by the cook's camp and pick up food for your trip back."

"Yes, Sir, General. Thank you. We will no doubt have to look for General Marion because he was off to deal with your other orders when we came across Rufus and his two friends. We will be sure to give him your regards, General."

With that, the boys went off to gather the supplies that would be needed before they could reach Marion and the rest of the militia. Within a matter of minutes, they were waving goodbye to General Greene and heading out to catch up to their commander.

Chapter 21

Meanwhile, Lt. Colonel Watson had broken away from the plantation that he had been using for a sanctuary, and was hastening to Georgetown, where he hoped to find help and safety for his troops. Learning of Watson's movement toward Georgetown through one of his own spies, General Marion was now leading his militia toward the Sampit River, which Watson would have to cross in order to reach Georgetown. As before, Marion sent a party of horsemen ahead to destroy the bridge crossing the river, hoping to slow Watson down and overcome him.

Upon arriving at the Sampit River crossing, the dragoons realized that, again, a bridge had been destroyed. "What shall we do now, Colonel? As you can see, the bridge has been destroyed!"

"We must get across this river! Marion is on our tail and he will destroy us, too, if we can't reach Georgetown as soon as possible!" Watson responded. "So, men, take all you can carry on your horses and get across that river by any means!"

"Yes, Sir," replied his officers, as they issued orders to their soldiers.

As Watson's desperate troops splashed and plunged into the frigid water, one of the soldiers called out, "Colonel! The rebels are upon us!" Just as he said those words, Marion's forces started shooting and yelling.

"Head them off, men!" Marion yelled. "We need to keep those men from threatening us anymore. Onward, lads!" That was all the militia needed to hear as they chased Watson's troops into the river.

As the British scrambled across the river and to the other side, several of Watson's troops were killed. The Tories panicked and fled from the scene. Even Colonel Watson's horse was shot out from under him, but the colonel himself, was left unscathed. In total, twenty of the British were killed, and thirty-eight were wounded, while General Marion lost only a single soldier, whom he mourned, as was his wont to do over a lost man.

"That appears to be the end of this battle, General," Peter Horry said as he surveyed the area. "All we can see now is that Watson is loading his wounded men into their remaining wagons and heading to Georgetown," he continued.

"Let them go," sighed Marion. "This rout has humiliated him as we were a much smaller unit of fighting men than he had. Hopefully, this will keep the British out of this part of South Carolina for a while. Let us head back to Snow Island and get some peace for a while. We are in need of a good break for a few days. I expect that General Greene will have more orders for us soon enough."

"Yes, General," agreed Peter. "I am ready to head back to a safe and secure place for a while. I am anxious to meet up with Hugh to see what he has accomplished since we have been here. I think that we will probably meet him on the way back to Snow Island. Also, Will and Thomas should be back with us by now. Where do you think they are? Surely General Greene didn't make them stay with him after they dropped off Rufus!" He exclaimed.

Marion was wondering the same thing because both Thomas and Will had become two of his favorite young men. They were always on the ready to do whatever he suggested. There was nothing that signaled fear in their eyes whenever they were sent on a mission. They just did it!

As the militia filed into an orderly column and started on their way back to their encampment, Marion was relieved to see the two boys headed toward him. As usual, they were barreling toward him with some kind of news that might be good or bad. "What now?" He wondered, for the boys did not look too happy. He dreaded hearing what they had to say. It couldn't be good news according to the looks on their faces.

The boys saluted their commander as the horses drew nearer to each other. Thomas spoke first this time. "Sir, we just met Colonel Horry and he told us that our camp had been destroyed again while you were battling with Colonel Watson. Apparently, Colonel Doyle made good on his threat to find your camp, Sir, and destroyed it."

Will jumped into the explanation. He added, "Sir, Colonel Horry said that Doyle had burned or dumped all the weapons, ammunition, and stores into the surrounding rivers, and there is nothing left of that base on Snow Island. When we met Colonel Horry, he was on his way to catch Doyle."

Marion sighed. After taking six months to gather all of those supplies, he couldn't believe that they were now all gone, totally destroyed. But, not letting this setback get him down, he called out to his brigade. "All right, men. Let's join Colonel Horry and see if we can catch that Doyle before he escapes!"

Immediately, everyone turned their horses around and followed their commander, as he headed in the direction that Thomas and Will had mentioned. Marion was determined to encounter Doyle and get retribution for the damage he had done on Snow Island.

Finally catching up with Horry, Marion worked with his colonel to figure out a way to stop the British in their tracks. Unfortunately, Doyle had already decided to burn his baggage because he wanted to get safely away from the Americans. This he did, and fled to Camden looking for protection from his enemy.

"Well, Hugh, it looks like Doyle has hightailed it out of here. After finding all of what remains of his supplies, I think that in order to reach safety he had to leave everything that was not necessary for his troops. I doubt if we will see him near here again, so let's return to Snow Island and see what we can salvage. Before we do that, though," continued Marion, "I want to talk to the men. Have them all come forward so that I can speak to them."

"Yes, Sir," said Hugh. "I will pass the word along to the men. While you are speaking to the militia, Sir, shall I have Thomas and Will go ahead to scout out the area and make sure no British are left near the island?"

"Yes. That sounds good, Hugh. What I have to say to the men won't affect those two boys, anyway.   Go ahead and send them back to our last base. They are always ready to do something, so let's keep them busy. They do seem to enjoy being a part of this militia."

Leaning out of his saddle, Horry stretched his neck to see where the boys were located in the line. Spying them near the front of the file, he beckoned them to come forward. "I wonder what Colonel Horry wants," mused Thomas. "Let's see if we are needed to deliver a message or something." Spurring their horses on, they quickly reached Colonel Horry's side. "Do you need us, Sir?" He questioned the colonel.

"Yes, men. General Marion wants you to ride on ahead and check to make sure no British soldiers have stayed around to ambush the column. Remember to keep your heads down, muffle your horses' feet and keep them muzzled until you are safely back at camp. If you see anything amiss, come back and let the general know. Just be as safe as possible."

"Will do, Colonel," Will stated. The boys proceeded to dismount from Ebony and Saucy. As they pulled out their leather mufflers and began to cover their horses' hooves, General Marion approached them and warned them to be diligent in watching their surroundings. They assured him that they would, and as soon as they were finished, they waved to the general and rode off in the direction of Snow Island.

In the meantime, the rest of the men had brought their horses close to Marion, so that they could hear what he had to say. They were all curious to know what would be happening.

"Men, I know that we have been on the road for many days and you are all battle-weary. I am giving you an opportunity to return home to check on your families to make sure everything is well with them. Tend to your farms and livestock, for this is your reason for fighting the British—so that you can still have your own land and not have to bow down to the British needs, wants, or desires. I would ask that you not all go at the same time, however, as there is still much to be done before we will be free."

"Please speak to the major or Colonel Horry if your desire is to go home for a while. They will let me know of your decision. Take care until you are called upon again." The men shifted in their saddles and murmured their thanks to their commander.

As Thomas and Will rode stealthily along the path toward camp, they watched and listened carefully for any signs of the enemy. They were about three hours ahead of Marion's militia when they heard galloping hoofbeats coming toward them. Unsure of who was heading their way, they pulled off to the side of the road to see who was in such a hurry. They recognized Simon, the horse handler, whom Marion had sent on an errand to General Greene.

"Whoa! Hey, fellows! What are you doing out here ahead of the main brigade?" Simon called out to Thomas.

"Where are you going in such a hurry?" Thomas asked.

Simon asked. "How far is the general from here? I have a message for him from General Greene."

"We were about three hours ahead of him and the militia," Will responded. "They may be closer than that since we have been taking our time scouting out the trail to make sure there are no British stragglers ready to pounce upon the men as they come by."

"Your horse looks pretty lathered up, Simon," said Thomas. "Our mounts are still fairly fresh as we have been riding slowly toward the camp. Would you like us to deliver this message for you, so that you can rest yourself and your horse?"

"Thanks, men. That would be great! We have been riding at breakneck speed all day to get this letter delivered. I am surprised that my horse hasn't floundered, yet. He has good stamina but I don't want to ask him to run at a full gallop for the next three hours. Snow Island is not far away and I should be able to make it there soon, even if I go at a slower pace."

"Be forewarned, Simon," said Thomas. "Colonel Horry informed us earlier that our camp is now a shambles, thanks to Colonel Doyle and his men. So, just be careful when you go in. The rest of us won't be too far behind at that point."

"Oh, no!" Simon exclaimed. As he trotted away, he called back over his shoulder, "I will try to clean up the camp while I'm waiting for you."

"Okay," the boys answered as they sped back to deliver the message from General Greene. Within an hour and a half, the boys came upon the militia. They saluted the general and told him that they had a message for him from Greene. They explained about Simon and that he had gone on ahead to the camp to see what he could do to prepare for the militia's return.

"Let me have that letter, Thomas," Marion said as he held out his hand to receive it. He signaled to Colonel Horry and Major James to come forward as he read the missive. "It appears, men, that General Greene and his army are planning to come back to South Carolina, and he wants us to meet up with Colonel Lee at Black River. Our brigades, together, are to take the British forts between Charleston and Camden."

Major Jones said, "How much help will we be, Sir? We have only about eighty men left to fight, since the others have returned home for a rest."

"We will do whatever we can with what we have. In the meantime, let us see what supplies we can garner from the Patriots who usually keep us in food, guns, and ammunition."

"Aye, aye, General! We are on our way," responded his officers, as they pivoted on their horses to speak to their individual units.

As the men prepared to go, General Marion added, "Since time is of the essence, try to be back at Snow Island by tomorrow this time. Twenty-four hours should be enough time to get what we need. We have no idea how long we will be gone from the encampment, so get as much as you can. I will take a few of the boys and head out to the old base and see what Simon has been able to do. Meet us there in twenty-four hours. I will be taking Thomas and Will with me as scouts, and a few of the other men as well."

"Yes, General," they answered.

"Thomas and Will, lead out. I want you boys to scout out the trail as we get closer to camp. Whistle if you see or hear anything out of the ordinary. Stay within a half mile or so of us. We will be following at a slower pace in order to give our animals an opportunity to recoup their energy and strength. Watch for British soldiers who might be stragglers or some who have been conveniently left behind to accost us. And, of course, there are always the Tories to look for behind every bush."

Snickering, the boys saluted and rode off, hoping that they might surprise any enemies hidden along the wayside. As they observed the sky, they noticed that a beautiful sunset was beginning to form. The reds, pinks, blues, and purples added a surreal glow to the landscape around them. Pretty soon, though, darkening shadows would follow them back to the swamp, so they needed to be watching carefully to make sure that those shadows were not moving on two legs.

Chapter 22

Trotting nonchalantly down the trail, Thomas and Will were surprised to see Simon waiting for them just before they reached Snow Island. "What are you doing here, Simon?" Will asked.

"I ran into Buddy when I returned to check out our camp. He had already arrived and had been putting things back in order as much as he could. He was on the other side of the island when Doyle and his rogues tore up this camp. He returned shortly before I did, and was already getting together food supplies for the men. As we speak, he is preparing a meal for the general and the rest of the men."

"I am thankful that the general had the foresight to put up several camps on this island, so that if this ever happened, there would be another place for us to rest our weary bodies. While Buddy was cooking, I thought that I would just come out here to wait and guide you a different way into the camp. Where are General Marion and the rest of the militia, anyway? I thought that they would be with you."

"They are only about a mile behind us, so they should be arriving in the next few minutes. Have you seen any suspicious characters lurking around? We have been informed that there are Tories here still trying to find General Marion and his headquarters. Will and I have been scouting and have seen nothing of consequence."

"I haven't seen anyone who appeared out of place. In my experience, they seem to be fearful of Snow Island, the Tories anyhow. The soldiers, not so much, because they have to go where they're ordered."

Just as Thomas was about to respond, the sound of thundering horses' hooves sounded nearby. "There they are now," said Thomas. "The general is leading the way. Let's wait here, Will, until they reach us. Then, we can go on together."

"Ho, there, Will, Thomas, and Simon! How are things at the camp? Should we take the time to see if there is anything salvageable?" Marion asked.

"Yes, Sir," answered Simon. "Buddy is in the process of having a meal prepared, and between the two of us, we have made it habitable again, General.

By the time we arrive, everything should be ready for a meal and a good night's rest. How does that sound, Sir?"

"That sounds wonderful to my ears, Simon! Well done! Let's be on our way, then! I know that the men and horses are exhausted from all the fighting of the past few days. A good night's rest will be soothing to the soul as well as to the body."

Within the hour, all of the militia, both cavalry and infantry, were settled in at the restored camp. True to Simon's word, Buddy had a hardy meal prepared and every man ate his fill. Now, they were resting and relaxing on their blankets as they listened to the muted noises of the birds and animals in the surrounding swamp.

All but Francis Marion, that is. He was reviewing the letter that he had gotten from General Greene, asking him to join with Lt. Colonel Henry Lee at Black River. He wasn't sure what his eighty men could do, but since the general had requested his help, he was obliged to go. Knowing that Greene's requests were always urgent, Marion had decided to give his men a good night's rest, and then leave in the morning to meet up with Colonel Lee.

It was, now, well into April in 1781. The sun was beginning to pour its heat down on everybody in the South. Even on Snow Island, which was covered in masses of trees and bushes, the heat was almost unbearable. On top of that, the mosquitoes in the swamp were coming to life, and after a miserable night of oppressive heat and bugs, the men were happy to be up and on their way out of the swampy and muggy area.

By 6 o'clock, everyone was up and at roll call. Many more of the militia, who had left earlier to take care of their families, had returned in the middle of the night, so as not to arouse any Tories or Loyalists that might be on the lookout for Marion and his men. Now, they all busied themselves eating the pancakes and sorghum that Buddy had prepared for them before departing on another long trek.

General Marion was already on his horse, Bull, and was waiting impatiently for the men to complete their meals. After giving them another fifteen minutes, he called out, "Mount up, everyone! Colonel Lee is waiting for us and we need to be on our way. Make sure that you are fitted with all the supplies you need for the trip. Buddy and his assistants will follow later after the camp is cleaned. He will be bringing extra staples, guns, and ammunition in his wagon."

"Hugh, get your infantry together, and Peter, get your cavalry set up at the front of the line. Thomas and Will, I want you with me, in case I need to send a message to either Colonel Lee or General Greene."

"We're all set to go, General," responded the two young friends.

Thomas and Will directed Saucy and Ebony toward the general. "Stay close by me, men, as I might have need of you before this day is over."

"Yes, General," they replied. As they pulled their mounts in behind Marion, Thomas looked askance at Will. He whispered, "Maybe we will see some action today. I wonder which fort we will be attacking first."

Marion heard their whispering and said that they were heading first to Black River to meet up with Colonel Lee, and then head to Fort Watson which would be their first battleground.

Will said, "We weren't very successful on our first try at Fort Watson, Sir. Colonel Sumter lost eighteen men that time. Do you think we will have a better chance this time?"

"With our eighty men, counting the ones who had returned during the night, and Colonel Lee's brigade, we should be able to take Fort Watson without much trouble. But only time will tell," said Marion.

Their commander set a brisk pace throughout the day and everyone was feeling the strain as they neared Black River. Marion pulled Thomas and Will aside and gave them an oral message for Colonel Lee. "Tell him that we are close to his position and should be with him within the next few hours. Make it snappy, boys, as he is no doubt wondering what has taken us so long to meet up with him!"

"Yes, General Marion," they responded.

"Should we wait there for your arrival, or return and travel the rest of the way with you?" Will asked.

"No need to race your horses back here, men. They will be tired from all of the running around you have been doing today. Just wait with Colonel Lee until we get there and give your horses a well-deserved rest. We will see you soon. As always, keep your wits about you, your eyes open, and your ears attuned to every sound around you."

Nodding in acknowledgment of their general's comments, Thomas and Will started toward Black River to deliver his message to Colonel Lee. They kept on constant alert because they didn't know who or what might be lurking in the shadows. Even though the sun was out, their path was a dark passageway because of all the trees which made a natural canopy overhead. In this darkened area, eerie noises caused them to feel the hairs that were standing up on their arms and the backs of their heads.

Something must be causing this feeling, but what was it? They slowed their horses at this point, so that they could concentrate on their surroundings.

So far, during his time in the South with General Marion, Thomas had escaped injury and capture, but there was still time for anything like that to happen, so he kept his eyes trained on the roadside, scanning any area that might be suspicious. Will, while getting shot in the arm, also had escaped anything more dire. He, too, was watching out for any scurrilous men skulking around in the underbrush.

Suddenly, out of nowhere, came the words, "Halt! Get off your horses, throw down your pistols, and put your hands up! Do. It. Now!" Thomas and Will looked at each other and followed the orders given. While they were dismounting, out of the brush walked eight British regulars. Oh, boy! What had they gotten into? They had been so careful, watching for trouble, and here they were, right in the middle of it! What to do?

"What are you lads doing out here? We have been following you boys for a while, racing your horses along the road. We have had a hard time running to keep up with you. Thankfully, you slowed down and now we have you!"

Being a quick thinker, Thomas was about to answer, when Will spoke up. "We are on our way to my father's plantation, which is a few miles from here. My father is a loyal Tory and would not be happy to hear that you have apprehended us, and treated us as if we were the enemy!" He spouted.

"That may be so," the soldier stated, "but you still did not answer my question about what you are doing out here. You are mighty close to Snow Island, which is where that infamous Swamp Fox abides."

At this point, Thomas, knowing that he needed to divert these soldiers from Marion's men who would be along soon, spoke up. "We were trying to see how close we could get to Snow Island before we would be noticed by his militia. Surprisingly, we were able to get all the way to the island and couldn't find a thing there. It appears that the camp has been abandoned. There was no sign of the Swamp Fox or his militia. So, we were on our way to Mr. Francis's plantation to give him that message."

"Well, then, we will just accompany you back to the plantation and hear you give your explanation to your father, Mr. Francis! If he is as loyal as you say, then we will let you go on your merry way. Just hold on to the reins, walk your horses, and lead the way. We will keep your guns in safekeeping until we are satisfied that you are telling the truth."

What a mess, thought Will. He continued to ruminate on what his father would do when he arrived back home. *Father knows that I have joined the Patriot side. He will likely turn me over to the soldiers to be imprisoned if we go back to the plantation. But, how can we get out of this predicament? I need to speak with Thomas somehow, and decide what to do. And, we still have to get that message to Colonel Lee. At least we will be leading these soldiers away from General Marion and his men. But, right now, I need to talk with Thomas! How can I make that happen?*

That problem was taken care of for him by George, the corporal leading these British regulars. He called out, "Let's stop, men! We have been on the road for quite a while. Let's take a breather. Keep an eye on those two lads. We don't want them getting into trouble," he snickered. "Just put them over there by that magnolia tree. Then, we can stretch out for a few minutes of rest."

"Yes, Corporal," one of the men answered. "Shall we post a guard?"

"I don't think there's a need," said George. "After all, we have their weapons and their horses. They won't get very far without them in this dangerous part of the country."

So, Thomas and Will were led over to the tree, where they sat down close enough to each other to carry on a whispered conversation without being heard.

The soldiers all found places on the ground where they could stretch out. Thomas and Will looked at each other, both knowing that they had to come up with a plan, and very soon. "What can we do, Will?" Thomas whispered. "We have got to get that message delivered to the colonel."

"I know," said Will. "I've been thinking. Look at those soldiers! Those men are so weary, they'll probably fall asleep as soon as they close their eyes. They haven't left a guard to watch us or anything! Maybe we can sneak away while they are sleeping. The problem will be keeping our horses quiet while we do it."

"We will have to make sure they are sound asleep before we even move from this tree," replied Thomas. "At least they didn't tie us up. We just have to mask the noises from our shoes and the horses' hooves. We can forget about trying to find our weapons! They're probably in the possession of the corporal or one of the other soldiers."

As the boys looked around, they could see that some of the soldiers were already falling asleep and they could hear the snoring of a couple of the others. Impatiently, the boys thrummed their fingers on their legs, watching and waiting…waiting…waiting! It seemed like it was taking forever! They needed to be gone already!

Finally! It looked like the last man had fallen asleep. Now they could escape. Slowly, Thomas and Will stood up, very thankful that they hadn't been tied to the tree. As quietly as they could, they sneaked past the dozing soldiers. Trying to keep their balance while on tiptoe, they managed to find Ebony and Saucy. Fortunately, the horses were still saddled. Silently, the boys crept up to the muzzles of their horses and tried to keep them from nickering. Instead of leading their horses away, they decided to mount. They should be able to outrun men on foot!

No sooner had they gotten on their horses, when a shout from one of the soldiers alerted them to the fact that someone had not been sleeping as soundly as they thought. All of a sudden, a barrage of bullets whizzed past their heads. The boys spurred their horses on, keeping their heads low. Now they could hear all eight of the soldiers yelling for them to stop or be shot. They did not heed them but kept racing as fast as their mounts would go.

They were so frightened that those bullets would hit either them or their horses. They kept going! The angry shouts from the soldiers receded and they eventually felt safe enough to slow down.

"Whew!" They both exclaimed at the same time.

"I thought we were gonners!" Will said shakily.

"Me, too," muttered Thomas. "That was too close! Do you think that they will try to follow us?"

"I don't think so," answered Will. "They can't possibly catch us, so let's get turned in the right direction and deliver General Marion's message to Colonel Lee. After being stopped by those soldiers, we have lost at least an hour of time. Fortunately, the soldiers were too tired to take us too far down the wrong road. Let's stop for a minute and let our horses take a breather."

Dismounting, the boys looked their horses over to make sure all was well. When Will walked around Saucy, he noticed that she had been grazed on her right flank. There was a slow stream of blood coming out. "Aw, Saucy! You've been injured!" Will worried. "Come and see, Thomas. She's been shot!"

Thomas looked at Will's horse. Having grown up on a horse ranch, Thomas knew that he needed to take care of the graze so that it would not become infected. Because he never knew when he might need it, he always carried a special salve to put on Ebony's scratches and cuts. Locating the ointment, Thomas swiftly plastered it on Saucy's side. By this time, the bleeding had all but stopped, and so the salve stayed in place to do its job.

Sitting on the ground, Thomas and Will sighed in relief. Not only had they gotten away safely from the British, but they and the horses were able to get some needed rest themselves. Time was fleeting, though, so they couldn't spend too much time lollygagging around. After a few short minutes, they were up on their horses and off to find Colonel Lee.

Not realizing how close they had already been to the colonel, they were surprised to find themselves on the outskirts of his camp in short order. Explaining their reasons for being there, the guards finally let them through, and directed them to where the colonel's tent was.

Walking their horses to the colonel's temporary headquarters, Thomas and Will asked to be admitted to his tent. Explaining what had occurred, they gave Colonel Lee the message from General Marion. After being with Marion in an earlier campaign, Lee recognized the lads, and so listened intently to what they had to say. "I am really glad you got here with the message. I was wondering what was keeping the general from getting here sooner, per General Greene's orders. If Marion can get here by nightfall, we can leave for Fort Watson in the morning."

Chapter 23

General Marion and his men arrived at Lee's headquarters later that night, and after a full night's rest, both Lee's brigade and Marion's militia made for Fort Watson early the next morning. This fort was an important part of the British line of communications from Charleston, so the rebels knew that they had to clear it for General Greene. But only a few weeks earlier, Thomas Sumter and his followers had attacked the fort, and the British had withstood the assault and had been successful in killing many of Sumter's men, thereby keeping the fort under British control.

Thomas and Will knew the story of Sumter's defeat and it had crossed their minds that the same thing could possibly happen to them. They also knew that the fort was built on an old Indian mound that was much higher than the surrounding land, and thus easier for the British to defend. "How are we going to take this fort?" They asked each other.

Fort Watson was well-protected and defended, so Marion and Lee needed to come up with a plan. The fort, itself, was small, but its position was strong. Not only had the British placed three rows of felled trees with sharpened branches facing outward which would be a dangerous problem for anyone trying to invade the fort, but the British had also cleared away all trees and brush from around the fort, so that it might be easier to defend.

On top of that, Marion's and Lee's sharpshooters would not be able to have any cover from which to fire on the fort. It looked like an impossible task to both commanders. So, what to do?

Thomas noticed that those inside the fort had to come out to replenish their water supply. Obviously, there was no other water inside the fort that could be used, so he pointed that fact out to Marion and Lee. "Excellent!" Both men said.

"Good observation, Thomas," Marion said. "Let's post riflemen to pick off those soldiers who come out to gather water from the lake. That should give us more time to figure out how to take this fort away from them. We don't have any artillery with which to bombard the fort and our men will soon run out of ammunition. Let's put our heads together, men, and solve this problem as quickly as possible."

At about that time, Will and three other militiamen showed up. They had been sent by Marion earlier to spy out as carefully as possible what was going on inside the garrison. "Sir," whispered Will. "The soldiers have dug a well just outside the fort and they have put a covered wall around it to protect themselves. Now they don't have to go to the lake to get their water. What shall we do?"

"Right now, the only thing I can think of is to wait them out. They will run out of ammunition and food soon." While Marion was stating this fact, one of his officers came up to him and made a suggestion.

"General, what if we constructed something like a tower that would go higher than their fort? Then we could shoot down at them and pick them off one-by-one."

"How would we do that, Major Maham? They have cut down all the trees around us, so we would have to go further away from our location to get the wood. If we are able to do that, then how would we build it?"

"I have devised a way to do that, Sir." With that, the major pulled out a piece of paper upon which he had penciled a design. "If we put the logs crosswise like I have sketched, we can build it up and create a flat area at the top where marksmen could stand and shoot down onto the soldiers inside the fort."

"Hmmm," said Marion. "That sounds like a good plan. Major, I will put you in charge. Send out whatever men you need to gather wood to make this thing. Hopefully, it can be readied soon and we can get this eight-day siege over with. I have always been a man of action and it's been hard for me to just sit around waiting for something to happen. I would much rather be out attacking and ambushing the British than sitting here!"

"Yes, General. I will see to it all. If we have access to as much wood as needed, we might be able to finish it by nightfall," the major added.

The men were sent out to fall the trees from the nearby swamps and then chop them into logs, which did take some time to complete. But true to his word, after everything was cut and ready, the major had been able to erect the tower in a single night, and by dawn, riflemen were standing on the tower's platform, waiting to shoot down anything or anybody that moved.

In the meantime, Marion had the Patriots creep closer to the fort and start to rip apart the British defenses and the actual walls of the fort. He had Lee ready his infantrymen with fixed bayonets, so that they could charge the fort and finish off the plan. When everyone was in place, Marion issued another request for surrender.

As a result of the request, Thomas, who was on the high perch and watching for the enemy, was the first to see the white flag when the sun came up. He called out to the general. "Sir, look at the fort. There's a white flag being waved from the top of the wall. Does that mean what I think it means?" He asked.

Marion turned his head to see what Thomas was pointing at. His eyes widened and a big smile took control of his face. "That's exactly what it means, Thomas! Good eye! Let's see what they have to say." He commenced to walk closer, and to his amazement, he saw the British lieutenant standing near the soldier holding the flag. "Stay where you are, Lieutenant!" Marion ordered. "We will have our discussion right here."

"Yes, General. After eight days, I thought that you would have given up and left us alone, but I see that's not the case. When dawn came, my men were shocked to see a tower above them. They saw that your riflemen could shoot down into the stockade's interior and they feared for their lives. They have put down their arms and have refused to defend this fort any longer. So, when you issued the request for surrender early this morning, I had no choice but to comply. I only ask one thing, General, that you consider being merciful to my officers and men when you set your terms of surrender."

"Thank you for surrendering before we had to come in and possibly kill more of your men or have any of my men shot down. I will speak to Colonel Lee about your request and I will get back to you. In the meantime, my soldiers will be rounding up all of the stockade's men, ammunition, and other necessary supplies." Saying that, Marion walked away to meet with Lee to consider the surrender terms. Thomas and Will stepped to either side of the general in a protective stance as he walked toward his militia.

"Colonel Lee," he called. "Let's have a discussion about what we should do with this enemy garrison and its defenders." Lee moved to Marion's side and together they bandied ideas back and forth. The first item on the agenda was to take all ammunition, guns, and food supplies, and then destroy the fort so that it was no longer usable to the enemy. Next, they discussed what to do with the soldiers and the Tories. The officers, receiving their orders, picked several men, including Thomas and Will, to load all ammunition and supplies into wagons, and then raze the fort.

Heading back to the British, who had now been rounded up, Marion and Lee nodded to the lieutenant, who cautiously approached them.

"We have come up with a decision that we feel is generous to you and your men," Marion said. "You, your officers, and your regulars will be paroled to Charleston to await exchange. You will also be allowed to keep your personal belongings and your sidearms. However, those traitorous Tory irregulars that you have with you will be held and treated as prisoners of war."

"Thank you, General Marion. That is very kind of you, and certainly more charitable than we expected. By your leave, General, I will speak to my men and explain the terms of their surrender. They will remain in order until you are ready to have us leave."

Marion waved the lieutenant off and then called out to Thomas and Will, who had been working in the fort. "Lads, I need you to carry a report to General Greene right away. Give me fifteen minutes, and while I am writing out the news, gear yourselves up for a few days' trip, as I am not exactly sure where the general is at this time. I do believe that he was on his way to attack the British at Camden but I'm not sure if he is there, yet."

"Yes, General," they responded, and off they went to do as he had ordered. Grabbing all the essentials they would need, Thomas and Will prepared themselves and reported directly back to General Marion within the allotted time.

"Here we are, Sir," Will announced as they approached Marion.

"So, I see," he answered. "You boys are always timely, and I like that."

"Thank you, General," Thomas said. "It is our aim to do whatever you ask as quickly as possible. And, now we are ready to deliver your message to General Greene if you have it for us."

"Here you are, men. Go quickly and safely because this area is still filled with Tories who supported the British dragoons at Fort Watson." Handing the report to Will, the general turned to go back to his tent. The boys, who had already muffled their steeds' hooves, climbed on their horses and trotted quietly from the area.

Once on the trail North, Thomas and Will put their horses into a full gallop, and as they did so, kept their eyes alert to any danger around them. "Will, you know this area better than I," Thomas said. "Which way to Camden?"

"If I recall," Will said, "Camden is almost straight North of our location. I think that we can be there in a few hours. It is not as far as we thought."

"Great! Let's get moving, then. As soon as we deliver this report, we can get back to General Marion. I am sure that General Greene will have more orders for our commander. How much longer do you think this war will go on, anyway?" Thomas asked. "As much as I enjoy the new friends I've made, I am anxious to get out of the battles and get home. I hope that all is well with my family, and I hope my brother is still well. He had been fighting the British in Vermont and I sure would like to know where he is right now."

"I feel the same way," responded Will. "I haven't seen my family in months and I am praying that they are well, too. I am sorry that my father and I are on opposite sides in this war, so I pray that it will be over soon, too, because I'm anxious to amend things with him."

Moving further down the trail, Will suddenly stopped.

"What's wrong?" Thomas asked.

"Look down the road, Thomas. There's a barouche turned over on its side. The wheels are still spinning, so this accident happened recently. Let's take a closer look." As the boys closed in on the carriage, Will's eyes grew wide. "That's my family's carriage!" He said.

"What happened? How did it get out here? Where is my father? What happened to the horses? Something's terribly wrong!" As he and Thomas were about to climb down off their mounts, they heard a groan come from inside the carriage.

Chapter 24

"What's that?" Thomas asked as he reached for his newly-received weapon, having lost his own to the British earlier. "There's something or someone in the carriage. Check it out, Will. I'll keep you covered."

Will hesitantly walked to the carriage and climbed up over the door to look into the window. What he saw saddened him. His father was lying on his side with blood streaming from his arm. "Help me!" The man muttered, not realizing that it was his son looking down at him from the window. His eyes were closed and Will could see that he was in a great deal of pain. The question now was how to get his father out of this predicament.

He climbed back down and strode over to Thomas. "Put your gun away," he said. "That's my father in there! He's been shot and his arm is bleeding quite a bit. We have to get him out, but first, we need to roll the carriage back over. We will have to do it carefully, otherwise he'll be hurt more."

"I'm so sorry, Will!" Concerned about the man, Thomas suggested, "Maybe we can use our horses to pull the carriage right side up, and then remove him so that we can tend to his wounds."

"Okay." Will gulped, his eyes filling with tears. "Let's get Saucy and Ebony closer to the carriage. Then, we can tie ropes to the top and pull it back so that the wheels are on the ground instead of in the air, and let's try to be quieter, since those renegades could still be near."

The boys did what they intended, and with a heave-ho, they had the carriage safely back on its four wheels. But while doing that, they had inadvertently caused more pain to the man within. "Let's hurry and get him out," whispered Will. Carefully opening the door, they rescued Mr. Francis from the eyesore that was the interior of the barouche. Everything was totally upside down!

As they carefully extracted him, Will wondered aloud. "I don't understand what happened here. My father is not even usually in this part of South Carolina, except when he goes to visit with General Cornwallis. Maybe he got lost on his way there and was waylaid by some villains."

"Possibly," said Thomas. "But let's get him taken care of first. Then we can ask what happened." The boys gingerly removed Mr. Francis's coat and looked at his arm. He had been shot, just as Will thought, but fortunately the bullet had gone all the way through his arm and out the back. Since Thomas always carried an emergency kit with him, they were able to stop the profuse bleeding by pressing some cloth against the wound.

The blood slowed to a small trickle and Thomas was able to bandage and bind the man's arm. After he bound the arm, Thomas continued to take care of the bruises and abrasions on the man's face. He had truly run into real trouble!

In the meantime, Will kept patting his father's face gently to get him to wake up and open his eyes. "Father, it's Will," he kept repeating. "I'm here! My friend and I are taking care of you. Wake up, Father! Please wake up! We need to ask you what happened and find out where your driver, Joe, is. Please, Father!"

As if coming back from a strange dream, or in this instance, a nightmare, Will's father slowly opened his eyes. He had a dazed look upon his face as if he couldn't remember where he was, what had happened to him, or who these two young men were who were hovering over him. Finally, he tried to speak, but it was more mumble than actual words. "Where am I, and what are you doing here, Will?" He asked. Will smiled in relief. At least his father recognized him. Now to find out what had transpired.

"Father," Will said. "We were on an errand for a friend when we saw a barouche on its side and came to investigate. We didn't know it was the family carriage until we got closer. We found that you had been shot and Thomas cleaned and bandaged up your arm. So, tell us what happened, if you can remember."

Mr. Francis's eyes cleared and he smiled up at his son. He continued to moan as he stated, "I have missed you so much, Will! It's so good to see you. What have you been doing? Your mother and siblings have missed you, too. I wish you would return home. It's boring without you around," he chuckled.

"Father, you know why I left, but let's discuss that later. Right now, I need to know what happened to you. Who shot you and why? Where are the horses? Where is Joe? I have so many questions!"

"Okay, son. First things first. I was on my way to Camden to take care of some issues. I am not sure why Joe took this route but here we are. As we were driving along, shots rang out, and the next thing I knew, Joe was lying on the ground, bleeding. I couldn't get out of the carriage, I was so stunned, and when I tried to open the door, I received a shot to my arm to encourage me to stay where I was. I looked out, and behold, there were six British dragoons. Four were on their horses, and the other two were unhitching my two horses with plans to ride off on them."

"I called out to them that I was friends with General Cornwallis and that he would hear of this travesty. They just laughed and shouted names at me, and before I knew it, the carriage was pushed on its side, and I couldn't get out with this hole in my arm. I was in pain from the bruises and scratches and I knew that I needed help for the gunshot wound, if nothing else. It's a godsend that you two boys came along when you did."

"This is one of the reasons that you and I have had a falling out, Father. I don't trust the British. They are cruel to everyone, not just the Patriots, even to their loyal supporters such as you. They have no loyalty to anyone but themselves. I will continue to feel that way until they are driven off American soil."

"I am about to agree with you, Will," said his father. "This whole affair has gotten out of hand. The line is drawn down the middle and it's hard to decide which side of the line we should be on. I have seen the atrocities of the British soldiers and I have also seen what the Patriots can do as well. I surely do want this war to be over soon, so that we can go back to a peaceful, civilized country again. But, right now, we need to find Joe and make sure that he is all right. Can you boys skirt along the sides of the road and see if you can find him?"

"Sure, Mr. Francis," Thomas replied. Pointing to one side of the road, he said, "You take that side, Will, and I'll take this side."

Scanning his side of the road, Thomas called out. "Will! Over here. There is some blood and it looks like something was dragged off the road into the woods."

Speeding to Thomas's side, Will looked at the blood and the marks. "Let's go into the woods, a little farther," Will said. "Maybe we can find Joe. Hopefully, he is still alive." Carefully examining the underbrush, Will spotted Joe lying on his back on the other side of a huge oak tree. "Thomas, Joe's over here!" He shouted. Thomas sped to his friend's side and knelt down by the injured man. He was still breathing, but the shoulder of his jacket was quite red from the loss of blood.

"Let's get him into the carriage with father," Will said. "We can hitch our horses to the carriage and drive them both to Camden. There should be a doctor in the town that can take care of them. We still have a message to deliver, but at the rate we're moving, General Marion might get to Colonel Lee before we deliver his message."

"Hold on, Will," said Thomas. "You do realize that Camden is still held by the British, don't you? We could be arrested!"

"I don't think that will happen, Thomas," he said. "We are just two boys who came across two wounded Tories and are bringing them in to see the doctor. When they realize who my father is, they won't bother questioning us. They'll just think that we are Tories, too. After all, rebels wouldn't dare to go into the enemy's lair, right?"

"We don't have to go right into the town, do we?" Thomas asked. "We can leave the carriage just inside the gate, explain our mission to the guard about finding these wounded men and that we were just bringing them in for medical help, unhitch our horses and leave. Couldn't we just do that?"

"We could," Will said, "but I would hate to just leave my father and Joe there in the carriage without escorting them to the doctor's office."

"You make a good point. It would be better to deliver them properly. There's only one thing, Will. You are used to being surrounded by British soldiers, Loyalists, and Tories, but I'll be scared to death! And shouldn't we take the feathers out of our hats?"

Will laughed. "You'll be fine, Thomas! Let's go and tell father our plan so that he knows what we are going to do."

"Won't he figure out that we are the enemy?" Thomas asked.

"I think he knows that already, Thomas. We have been wearing Marion's rebel sign in our hats and I am sure he's aware of what that feather means. He is a pretty smart man! I doubt that he will turn us over to the British, especially since he's not very happy with them right now. They did shoot him!"

The boys quickly outlined their plan with Mr. Francis. He assured them that all would be well and nothing horrendous would happen to any of them. He was quite certain that the soldiers who had injured him and Joe would receive their just dues, once he explained to the commander in charge of the garrison at Camden just what happened.

Will and Thomas needed to hurry in order to get their message delivered, so they quickly hitched their horses to the carriage and took off up the road to

Camden. Trying to miss ruts in the road, so that their passengers weren't in more misery, it took them another hour to finally reach their destination.

Greeting the guards at the entrance to the town, the two young men explained their situation, telling the guards that Mr. Francis was a close friend of General Cornwallis. Unhesitatingly, the two lookouts ushered them through the gates into the town and pointed them in the direction of the doctor's office.

After saying goodbye to his father, Will joined Thomas and together they slowly trotted out of the town, with no one being the wiser. As soon as they got far enough away from Camden, they flew as fast as their horses could travel toward Colonel Lee's location, which was only a two-hour trek. Upon arriving at Lee's headquarters, they were happy to see that they had arrived before General Marion.

After delivering the message and telling Colonel Lee why they were so tardy in bringing the report, he sent them to an area where they could get a much-needed respite for themselves and their horses.

Chapter 25

In the meantime, General Marion, himself, had gotten closer to his destination. Shortly after the lads had lain down and barely had their eyes closed, Marion and his militia arrived. Will and Thomas were awakened by the hubbub going on outside their tent. They recognized their commander's voice and immediately exited the tent to let him know that they had arrived and delivered his message to the colonel.

"Well, hello, men!" The general said. "I'm glad that you arrived safely. I have already spoken with Colonel Lee and he explained that you were delayed. I am sorry to hear about your father and surprised to learn that he had been attacked by his own people. I met him before the war and felt that he was a good man. I was sorry to hear that he had sided with the British, rather than the Patriots. But from what Colonel Lee told me, I understand that he might be changing his mind concerning which side of the war he may now be on. That is good news, indeed!"

"Yes, Sir!" Will responded. "I, too, am hoping that he decides we are the better side to be on."

"Well, come along, then," the general continued. "It seems that Colonel Lee has already received a request from General Greene that we should head toward Fort Motte and take it. From what I've heard rumored, it is the main British storehouse for supplies between Charleston and their forts further North in the state." That being said, the general walked back over to speak to Colonel Lee.

"Colonel Lee! Are you and your men all supplied and ready for another trek into British territory? General Greene seems to think that we make a pretty good team, and I think that I must agree with him," he chuckled. "My men and horses are tired from their long trip from Snow Island, so I would like to give them some time to relax and get everything together before our next foray into enemy territory. What do you say?"

"Since it is already late in the day, I suggest that we set out at dawn. That will give your men ample time to rest and refresh their supplies," stated Lee.

"Agreed, Colonel. And thank you for helping us with our provisions. We have had to parcel out just the necessary food items and ammunition for this trip. Thankfully, we were able to garner whatever we could find at Fort Watson for our use. I imagine that many of your own provisions came from the same source."

"You're right, General. They did. We do have a fairly good supply that you allowed us to confiscate, and I am willing to share those with you and your men. Let's go and make sure that things are allocated in the right way. Unfortunately, though we are on the same side, some of the Continentals still don't like the militiamen because of their supposed lack of training. I have seen your men in battle, Marion, and I have much respect for how they accomplish whatever you set them to do, without complaint, usually."

"I know that you have an issue with them leaving far too often, but the fact that their loyalty to the cause makes them come back, time after time, impresses me even more, especially those two young men who took care of two Tories, and then continued on to deliver your message to me."

"Will and Thomas are both very young but they have outdone more seasoned soldiers in many cases. What's more, they are fiercely loyal to the rebel cause and their willingness to do anything that I ask, regardless of the danger involved, impresses me greatly. They will make good leaders one of these days."

All this was said as the two commanders made their way to Lee's brigade and Marion's militia. They men were all milling around, wondering what was going on. They all stood at attention and looked toward their leaders, expecting some kind of explanation as to what they would soon be doing. Since the general was the one with the higher rank, Marion spoke first.

"Men," Marion began, "General Greene was so pleased with our results at Fort Watson that he wants us to continue to Fort Motte, and try to do the same thing there. That fort is about 30 miles from here, so it will take us about a day and a half to reach it. Colonel Lee and I have decided that we will start out early in the morning. That should give you plenty of time to rest and refresh your supplies."

The next morning, 6 May 1781, Lee and Marion marched their men toward their next destination: Fort Motte, the principal British supply depot for their fortifications farther North. This was a fort that the British did not want to lose. The fort, really a mansion belonging to Mrs. Rebecca Motte, the widow of a wealthy planter who had supported the Patriot cause before his death, was situated on a hill, with the stockade built around it. British officers had taken over the use of the mansion and had moved Mrs. Motte, her two daughters, and mother to the overseer's log cabin on the plantation grounds.

Still livid with the British for taking her home, Mrs. Motte, as soon as she heard that Marion and Lee were in the area, sent a note via her servant requesting that the two commanders make her cabin their headquarters during the siege. They very happily responded positively to her request.

Upon arriving at the fort, Lee and Marion were aghast to see that it was at least double the size of Fort Watson. It was still smaller than traditional fort standards, but the protective wall was made of sturdy wooden stakes, almost ten feet high, with blockhouses at the corners with openings for guns. It looked like it was going to be a formidable task to the Patriots. However, with a force of about four hundred soldiers between them, they felt that they could overcome the British who had less than half of that number.

Looking at each other, the two leaders thought of Thomas and Will immediately. Their eyes glistened as they discussed the best use of these two boys in this unlikely scenario. They would be the two who would take a flag of truce to Lt. Donald McPherson, the commander of the fort, when the right time came.

In the meantime, both Will and Thomas were helping the rest of the men dig zig-zagging trenches around the fort, so that they could get close enough to fire upon the soldiers inside the fort. Both lads were sweating up a storm as May started to become a very warm month and the sultry weather had begun. The plan was to dig the trenches closer to the fort and then bombard it with cannon fire.

But even with added slaves from surrounding plantations, they weren't able to dig fast enough. Lee and Marion had also received rumors that Lord Rawdon was bringing reinforcements to Fort Motte to aid the British soldiers who were inside.

Calling Thomas and Will to them, Marion and Lee told them that they were to take a message requesting surrender of the fort to the Americans. This was a first for the two boys, but they soldiered on, ever wary that they could be shot while out in the open.

Arriving at the gate, Will called out, "Ho, the fort! General Marion demands that you surrender this fort to him and Colonel Lee, immediately."

"Nay!" The reply came back from Lt. McPherson. "We will not surrender this fort today, or any day! Take that message back to your general!"

Receiving the report back, Lee and Marion knew that they had to take the fort the next day, or else give up and go back to General Greene. On top of that, Rawdon was fast approaching. They only had one option at this point. That was to burn down the mansion and the fort. They felt that the Patriot trenches were close enough to the fort so that they could shoot flaming arrows to the roof of the mansion. But in order to do that, they would need to inform Mrs. Motte of their plan to destroy her property.

So, now, here they were telling her what their plan was. "Go for it!" She said. "I'll even give you my East Indian bow and a set of arrows to help you out!" With her agreement, Lee and Marion planned to give the British one more chance to surrender. If they didn't, the mansion and stockade would be burned to the ground. So, the next morning, Will and Thomas approached the stockade again and asked for their surrender, and again, McPherson refused to give up the fort.

Thomas and Will returned to the trenches, where the soldiers were already preparing to fire arrows onto the house's dry, shingled roof. The roof was quickly aflame, and even though the British tried valiantly to douse the fire, the artillery fire from the Patriots kept them from succeeding. With nothing else to do, McPherson surrendered the garrison.

A loud hurrah rang out from the trenches as Will and Thomas led the men in shouts of glee when they saw the white flag of surrender hoisted. Then, the Americans entered the fort. While some doused the fire and saved the mansion, others took possession of the enemy's guns and provisions and demolished the rest of the fortifications.

That evening, Mrs. Motte invited the American and British officers to her cabin for dinner. While there, everyone was treated the same, and both Britons and Americans laughed and talked as brothers. Thomas and Will, not being officers, were not invited, but they could hear all of the goings on outside the walls where they had been stationed for security.

"Wow, Will! I wouldn't mind having some of that food in there. I can smell it through the walls," said Thomas.

"Me, too! I can hardly wait to get back home and have some of my mom's good cooking," said Will. "I can just taste her fried chicken, mashed potatoes, green beans, and gravy! Yum! What would your mom be cooking, Thomas?"

"She would be making her delicious corn chowder for our first course. Then we would have roast beef with mashed potatoes and gravy as well! It makes me hungry just to think about it. Hopefully, this war will be over soon and we can both go back to enjoying our moms' cooking."

"I would like to know where we will be going from here," said Will. "From what I have heard, the Americans have just about run the British out of the Carolinas and I am so glad! We have been doing a lot of fighting and I am tired and ready to go home. I wonder how my dad is doing, too, and if he's back home yet."

As the boys noticed that the noise in the house seemed to be settling down, Peter Horry rounded the corner of the house and relieved the boys of their duty, sending them to their beds for the night. They would all have to be up early for the formal surrender of the British to the Americans. Walking back to their bivouac tents, Will and Thomas observed that the trees were starting to bend as a sudden wind came upon them, blowing wildly. They feared that their beds would be blown away by the strong gusts of the gale.

Holding on to their hats, they scurried to their makeshift home, satisfied to see that they still had a place to sleep, at least for the time being. To their surprise, the wind died down as quickly as it had come upon them. The boys sighed with relief and quickly climbed into their beds, ready to put this day behind them.

Upon arising the next morning, the two young men were elated to see that General Greene had arrived during the night. He had come to see what had been done at Fort Motte and to congratulate both Marion and Lee on a job well done. Seeing Will and Thomas, he hailed them.

"Thomas! Will! How are you boys today? I am so happy to see that you arrived back in time to assist in the seizure of this fort. It has been a great success for our side. As I have already mentioned to Marion and Lee, you have all done a great job here. I certainly am proud of you both for your part in this. I will make sure to mention that in my next letter to your father, Thomas," the general said.

"Thank you, Sir," answered Thomas. "We have only done a small part, not worth mentioning," he said humbly. "But we have been glad to do our part. Isn't that right, Will?"

"Yes, that's right! It has been our desire to do our part for the cause, General, whatever it is," said Will.

"Well, you lads have done just fine. I know that I appreciate all the courier running you have both done between General Marion and myself. Things are starting to fall into place and we are hoping to end this war soon. I am sure that I will be seeing you young men again in the near future. Now, I must speak with your commander. Stay safe!"

"Yes, General," the boys replied. They watched Greene walk away and quietly call General Marion to his side. Marion ushered the general into his temporary quarters where Greene would likely give Marion and Lee their next missions.

"What do you think, Will?" Thomas asked. "Do you think it's that close to being over?"

"I guess the next few missions will give us a better idea but I know that the loss of this fort was a great blow to the British, since it was a major storehouse for all their guns, ammunition, foodstuffs, and other necessities," responded Will.

In the meantime, General Greene was talking to Marion and Lee, splitting them up again, so that Lee could go and assist Sumter in his mission to take Fort Granby. This left Marion on his own to continue harassing the Tories and British.

However, Marion still had Georgetown on his mind. He was hoping that General Greene would give him permission to launch another attack on Georgetown, a region full of Tories who were causing trouble for the loyal Patriots in the area.

Chapter 26

It had been a few days now since Fort Motte had fallen and word had come back to General Marion that the garrison at Orangeburg had surrendered to Colonel Sumter, while Lee had accepted the British commander's surrender of Fort Granby. Marion requested that General Greene allow him to take his militia to Georgetown and take that British holding. He and Lee had been unsuccessful when they tried before, but now he felt that he would have a better chance at overcoming the British there.

Meanwhile, Marion and his band of men had established themselves at a new hideout as their main Snow Island headquarters had been demolished. They were still within the defensive covering of marshes, cane brakes, and trees, and as before, on Snow Island, sentries had been posted all along the way to whistle or give bird calls signaling that there were strangers in the area, which reminded everyone to be on guard.

Not having heard a specific yes from General Greene about his several requests to move on Georgetown, Marion was beside himself. He knew that if the militia did not act soon, they might lose the opportunity to take another British stronghold.

General Greene finally gave a less than enthusiastic response to Marion a conditional approval, but only if Marion could be around to back up Sumter at Fort Ninety-Six, if the need arose. Marion was overjoyed! He took Greene's conditional agreement to be a 'Yes', so off he went to let his underlings know what was afoot. He was determined to take Georgetown!

Collecting his militia, Marion prepared to start toward Georgetown. Because he had such successful missions lately, many of his former men returned to him and added much-needed numbers to the militia. Sending his two young militiamen to scout out the area, he felt enlivened by the possibility of winning Georgetown this time. When Thomas and Will returned with knowledge that Georgetown was undermanned, he wasted no time in getting to the garrison.

After a day's travel, Marion and the militia arrived outside of Georgetown. As he did at Fort Watson, he decided to dig trenches around the garrison. Will and Thomas were given the jobs of standing lookout while the men worked in the trenches. Thomas laughed when he saw the fake cannons rolled up to the front of the lines. Marion had the men strip trees and paint them black to look like cannons. Maybe that would help frighten the men inside the garrison to give up without a fight.

Apparently, that was enough, for the commander of the garrison had all the cannons in the city spiked, boarded the soldiers and Loyalists within the city onto their ships, and then left the city the same night the siege began. Not a shot was fired! Georgetown had finally fallen to the Patriots and was now theirs! Thomas and Will added their hoorays to the cacophonous sounds coming from the rest of the militia.

"Well, boys," the general shouted. "Let's go inside and see what damage has been done to this town. We will confiscate everything that the Loyalists have left and use it for our own good. I need some new clothes, anyway, so let's move on in. I urge you to be careful, in case there is a Tory left who doesn't want to give up the garrison without a fight."

"Yes, Sir," the men responded with a gleeful shout as they entered the garrison. Having some time to themselves, Thomas and Will wandered around the town, ogling everything in sight. They hadn't been in a town for a while, so they took their time looking around. Of course, a good share of supplies had been taken to the ships by the Loyalists when they left, so the only real thing left to see or do was to dismantle the fortifications, and this would be a priority after a surrender.

The local Patriots cheered the militia as it took over the town. They were so glad to be rid of the Redcoats! Georgetown would no longer be a storage place for British soldiers and it would never again be a stopover and supply house for British forces.

After the men had received some leisure time, the order was sent to all the militia to meet in orderly fashion on the parade ground. There, they were given specific orders for the tear-down of the garrison. After all abandoned supplies were collected and divided evenly, the men were sent to various parts of the fortifications to begin dismantling. The barricades, themselves, were torn down and burned so that the British could no longer have use of them if they should return.

The spiked cannons would be left alone, since it would be a timely process to unspike them. Since citizens would return to their homes and businesses after the battles of war had ended, most structures were left unharmed.

The following day, the exultant Marion chose Thomas and Will to take the mandatory dispatch to General Greene to inform him of the fall of Georgetown. He sent them to get their gear together and then told them to return for his letter to the general. As excited as ever to be serving General Marion, the two boys rushed out of the fallen garrison to find their mounts which were picketed outside the town. Knowing that General Greene was at least three days' ride away, the boys got together all of the food, ammunition, and supplies that would be needed for the trip.

Then they hastened to Marion's temporary quarters, those of the previous commander of the garrison, where they were told to hurry to General Greene, but, in the meantime, continue to watch each other's backs.

Heading in a Northwesterly direction, the boys headed off to locate General Greene and deliver General Marion's message to him. Not wanting to tire their horses, Thomas and Will struck a leisurely pace along the woodsy path leading from Marion's quarters. Since much of South Carolina had now been subdued by the Americans, except for the Charleston area, the boys were not as vigilant in watching the area around them. They began conversing about what they would do once the war was over.

Will stated, "I will be going back home to my father's plantation when this is all done. What about you, Thomas?"

"I will return to my father's horse ranch and continue helping train the new yearlings that we get every year. Horsemen all over the colonies bring their yearlings to us to saddle train because they know my father and brothers are the best around when it comes to horseflesh," responded Thomas proudly.

"I would also like to continue my education," Will said. "I would really like to get into law, but I certainly don't want to go back to England to study, and as far as I know, there are no established law schools in America right now. Well, I am only seventeen, so maybe by the time I'm ready for that, a law school might be founded. Who knows?"

"I'm sure you would make a great lawyer, Will, especially with all of the experience we are getting in dealing with those who are opposite the law," stated Thomas. "In the meantime, I'm sure that your father will find plenty for you to do on the plantation. Anyway, didn't you have tutors? My brothers and

I had tutors because our farm was so far away from Boston. The only schools around us were for younger children."

"I did have a tutor," said Will, "but I learned just about everything he could teach me." He let out a huge sigh of frustration. "One of these days, Thomas, I will see you up in Boston. Maybe, I will get to defend you for some breakage of the law," he said, laughingly.

"Oh, please, Will. Don't get me started. My brothers already think that I get into too much trouble as it is. Just wait till they hear about my adventures down here with you, the militia, and General Marion. They will be amazed!"

"Speaking of the militia," Will said. "What do you think they are up to right now?"

"Probably on their way to Ninety-Six to meet up with General Green," answered Thomas. "I wish we were with them but we need to get this letter delivered as quickly as we can, preferably before General Marion arrives. He is depending on us."

This was the trend in their conversation as the two boys loped along, staying as close to each other as possible, so that they could continue talking while they were riding. So deeply were they following each other's train of thought, that they were not as careful in watching their surroundings. Suddenly, out of nowhere, there came a shout!

Chapter 27

"Halt!" Someone yelled.

Startled by the command, Thomas and Will looked around but couldn't see anyone. What on earth? They knew that they hadn't been watching as diligently as they should have, so anyone could have crept up on them unawares. Now, what was going on? They hadn't spotted any Red-or-Greencoats as they were riding along; otherwise, they would have taken some measures to protect themselves from any enemy lurking nearby.

"Who could that be?" Will asked. "I heard that there were some small Tory militias still roaming about, trying to disrupt our cause, but I didn't think they were this close to Georgetown. When we rousted the British garrison, I thought that all the Tories left with them."

"I know," answered Thomas. "I thought that, as well, and looking around, I still don't see anyone."

As quietly as a snake slithering out of the underbrush, two men dressed in homespun and carrying muskets stepped out from behind a large tree. They looked to be more criminal than loyal soldiers to a cause. Thomas and Will were immediately on edge.

As the men walked closer, the older one asked, "Well, who do we have here?" Looking closely at the two boys, he added, "They are dressed as we are but I don't recognize either one. Do you, Jed? I don't think they're from around here, so they must be strangers, and don't realize that they have wandered into our domain," he sneered.

Jed answered. "Nah! I don't know them. They look like they're up to no good to me. Wouldn't you say so, Jimbo?"

"Ah, yes! I reckon these two are spies, come to find our camp and tell our enemies where we are," responded Jimbo. "What say we take them with us and let Mr. Sykes ask the questions? He'll get every bit of information out of them, if I know him." He grinned as if he knew something that the boys didn't know about their leader. His yellowed teeth and filthy clothes did not bode well for the two boys. These men didn't look like they were on any side, but their own.

"Now, you just wait one minute! We are just two lads on a trip to visit a friend who fell out of a tree while he was trying to rescue a lady's cat. He was badly injured and we were just going to see how he was doing. Do we look like we have any information that would help you in any way?" Will asked. "We don't know who you are or where you live. We don't even care! All we have with us are a few supplies to carry us over during this trip, nothing more."

"A likely story," said Jed. "Let's just see what you have in those saddlebags! We can probably use just about anything you have in there," he said as he walked toward the boys. "Open up those saddlebags and let me have a look-see!" He commanded.

Thomas and Will, who were still seated on their horses, slowly undid the clasps to their saddlebags and let Jed look in. He pulled out everything—food, shirts, pants, ammunition, and eating utensils, but nothing else. Fortunately, Thomas had put the letter and his paper currency into a secret pouch sewn into the crown of his hat, and both boys had left their feathers with Simon, who would return them when they met up again. So, as far as they knew, nothing that they had would connect them in any way to the Swamp Fox.

Disgusted with finding nothing truly useful, Jed shrugged his shoulders and glanced at Jimbo. "They have nothing but a few bullets," he sighed. "I was hoping for something more substantial. These boys don't look any richer than we are. They only have a few pence between them. They can't even buy a glass of milk with the amount of money they have."

"Well! Let's take them to Sykes, anyway. They might have some kind of useful information," said Jimbo. "All right, boys. Get off your horses and lead them. Follow me," ordered Jimbo. "Jed, you walk behind them. We don't want them scurrying away, now, do we?"

Letting out sighs of frustration, the two boys walked along with the men who were probably outlaws wanted by both sides in this war. They feared that they would find out soon enough. They still had a message to deliver and time was flying away. Their only hope was to escape, somehow. They didn't want the men to find out that Will's father was a wealthy plantation owner, or they might be kept for ransom. Both boys, without conferring with each other, kept their mouths shut and didn't make a peep as they followed the other men to their erstwhile camp.

After a fifteen-minute walk, they arrived at their destination, hidden deep in the woods. Several roughly-dressed men with scruffy beards looked up as

Jimbo and Jed entered the camp with their two captives. Some of the men had been whittling with some ugly-looking knives. The hair on the boys' scalps stood on end as they surveyed the poorly maintained camp.

"This can't be good," whispered Will to Thomas as they surveyed their surroundings. "These men don't appear to be soldiers or militia. It looks like we have fallen into the hangout for a gang of thieves," he continued.

"Hey! Stop that whispering!" A man yelled. As Jed and Jimbo sidled over to him, the boys assumed that this man must be Sykes, their ringleader. "Who are these boys and why did you bring them here to our hideout?" Sykes asked.

"Their horses looked so grand, we thought that they would be carrying money or something else that could be useful to us, but their saddlebags were only carrying their necessities," Jed answered.

As that answer didn't seem to help Sykes' rancor, Jimbo jumped into the conversation and said, "We thought that they might have information we could use to help put us on the good side of either the British or the Patriots. If there were anything important to glean, we knew that you would be able to get it out of them," he added.

"All right, then. Let's see what they know, if anything. They are only just boys by the look of them. Bring them to my tent."

"Yes, Mr. Sykes," they both said. Hurrying over to Thomas and Will, they grabbed both boys by the arms and hustled them across the way to the leader's tent. "You'd better answer all his questions and tell him what you know, if you don't want to get beaten," said Jeb.

The boys gulped. Whatever could they tell this man that would help to keep themselves from getting beaten? Nothing much because they didn't have any knowledge that they could give to this group without betraying the general and the militiamen who were their friends.

Sykes stared at them with steely eyes, making Thomas and Will shiver anew. "Who are you two boys and what are you doing so far away from town? Are you looking to get into trouble, or what?"

"Sir," Will answered. "As we told Jimbo and Jeb, we are going to spend a few days with a friend who was injured when he fell out of a tree. He broke both legs and an arm and hasn't had any contact with us for a few days. We are worried that something worse has happened to him. His name is Steven Scott and he lives on a farm close to the North Carolina border. We have nothing of value that would help you and as you can tell by our belongings, we have very little money. We were hoping to just find folks who would share their barns with us on our trip to the Northern part of this state."

Pointing his finger at Thomas, Sykes asked, "Who are you and where are you from? You don't talk like any Southerner I know."

"You're correct, Mr. Sykes. I am from up North. I just came down to visit my cousin, Will, here, a few weeks ago. Then we heard that our mutual friend, Steven, fell from a tree a few days ago. Now, we are on our way to see him and help cheer him up," continued Thomas.

"Well, tell me this. Have you seen any activity on your trip North? Any of Marion's militia or British dragoons?"

"No," said Will. "Everything has been quiet. You wouldn't even know there was a war on where we've been. Of course, we've been trying to stay out of everyone's way, and except for you and your men, we have seen no one for the past two days. So, Sir, there is really nothing we have to offer you. Could you please let us continue our trip to see Steven?"

"Now, that's a good question. You are both hardy, healthy-looking young men, and I do need a couple more hands in the gang. I think you two would fit in nicely! Maybe I could sell you to the British Navy. They are taking all able-bodied young men they can find to fill in for those lost in battle. What do you say, men? Should we keep them or sell them?"

Mixed answers came from the gang members. 'Sell them!' 'Keep them!'.

Sykes said, "I can't say that I like the way that the British soldiers have tossed our families off their land, so why should I give them two good men? Nah! I think we'll just keep you young fellows."

"Oh…no…please…Sir!" Will stuttered. "Steven will be wondering where we got to and our families will be worried when we don't return home! Can't you just let us go? Please?"

"How about we let you make the decision? The gang will win no matter what you boys decide." Guffawing, Sykes said, "You can stay here with this upstanding and trustworthy group of men or be on a British ship doomed to be sunk by the time this war is over. It matters not to us. Either way, we will get some good-spending British cash or two new hands to help us in our endeavors. So, boys! What's it going to be?"

"Can we have a few minutes to discuss this?" Will asked.

"Why not? We have all the time in the world. We're not going anywhere," laughed Sykes.

While the whole gang watched them, Will and Thomas stepped away from Sykes to get a little privacy. "This is terrible," whispered Will. "What shall we do? If we are handed over to the British, we will no doubt be recognized by someone as being a part of Marion's militia and then we'll be hung for sure. But if we stay here, we will be involved with criminals."

"However, if we stay here," said Thomas, "we would have a better chance of getting away."

"That's true," agreed Will. "So, here we'll stay and look for a time when we can slip away."

"All right, boys. Your time is up. What's your decision?" Sykes asked.

"We have decided that staying on land is the better option," responded Will.

"Good choice," laughed Sykes. "We'll have you trained to do hold-ups, pick pockets, and steal from farmers in no time," he said.

"I don't think so," muttered Thomas under his breath.

"Jimbo! Jed!" Sykes called. "Since you captured these two, it's up to you to guard them and teach them the ropes. Make sure that they know the rules of this camp, too, and tell them what happens if they disobey or try to escape!"

"Yes, Sir!" The two men said. "We'll show them where to bed down and go over the rules with them. We'll pasture their horses along with the few that we have," added Jed.

"Good! And hurry up about it. We have plans to make!" Sykes ordered.

When the other men shifted their attention to their leader, Will and Thomas threw their bedding on the ground. Softly, Will spoke. "I wonder what those plans will include. Probably, something just as dishonest as forcing us to work with them. We've got to think of a way to get out of here, Thomas, and get this letter delivered to General Greene. What a mess we're in!"

"We have to get out of here tonight," Thomas responded. "General Marion is expecting us to complete our mission and General Greene is probably wondering why he hasn't heard from Marion already!"

Not full-fledged members of the gang, the boys were not expected to take part in the planning that was going on, so they sat alone on their beds discussing the best way to get free. "What possible way can we escape from here?" Will asked. As they were pondering the question and possible answers, Jimbo stomped over to them.

"Pick up your gear and go get your horses," he ordered. "Since we do our best work at night, Mr. Sykes is having us move to that small plantation up the road and check it out for anything valuable. We will stay on the outskirts, watching the action during the day, and then tomorrow night, we will strike. So, gather up your bedding and gear and go get your horses. We will be leaving in the next half-hour. So glad you fellows decided to join us," he chortled.

"Don't forget! We will have our eyes on you the whole time, so don't think of escaping." With that, he left to speak to the other men in the group.

"Now's our chance!" Thomas whispered. "Our horses are fast. Maybe we can outrun them!"

"We have to watch and see if they are going to put a guard on us," Will whispered back. "If they don't, we might chance it. If they watch us closely, getting away will be a little harder. We will have to wait and see what happens and bide our time. Let's just get Ebony and Saucy ready like they told us."

Quickly, the boys got their few possessions together and headed to the fenced-in area where their horses were pastured. The horses greeted them with welcoming nickers and moved toward the boys. Thomas and Will hugged their mounts and led them back to the camp. They didn't notice anyone following them, so they assumed that they were going to be left on their own without anyone guarding them.

They were too close to the camp to make their escape, yet. Hopefully the time would come soon. Wearing stoic looks on their faces, they walked back into camp.

When they entered, Sykes called out, "Well, you have stayed. We expected you to hightail it out of here as soon as you got your horses. We didn't have to shoot you after all. I guess we can trust you boys to stick to your word. Jed, call in Harry and Sam. They won't be needed to snipe at the boys."

Thomas and Will looked at each other. "Boy, it's a good thing we didn't take off like we wanted to," they mouthed to each other. "It looks like we would have been shot!"

Sykes already had his men lined up, so the two boys just joined in at the end. "Move quietly, everyone. It will take us a while to get there but we don't want to alert anyone who might send off a shot to warn others."

As the boys crept stealthily along with the rest of the gang, Thomas and Will tried to sneak further back in the line. They allowed the faster men to go on ahead, while they lingered slowly behind, waiting for an opportunity to withdraw from the whole group without being noticed. They saw a long bend in the path ahead and decided that this was the best opportunity they would get. They slowly climbed onto their horses, keeping their heads down, and hardly breathing in case someone would hear them. As the men kept walking along in the dead of the night, without many stars or the moon to be seen, Thomas and Will walked their horses slower and slower.

Finally, the men ahead of them turned the corner and the boys saw their chance to escape. Quietly turning their horses in the other direction, the boys urged their mounts to gain speed. They had no idea where they were going but the faster they got away, the better.

Within a few minutes, they heard yelling and gun shots from behind them.

They had been found out! "I think we can outrun them," Will shouted, "but we have to get farther away before we can find a place to hide. They know this countryside better than we do. So, let's hustle!"

"I'm right with you," agreed Thomas. "I don't hear anything right now. Sykes must have reminded them to be quiet. We need to keep our eyes and ears open, though, to make sure they don't creep up on us!"

An hour later, Will and Thomas decided that they had outrun their captors. Now, the question was, 'Where were they?' Thomas had been used to following the stars in his native New England, so he looked up at the sky. Fortunately, the clouds had lifted and he could make out the stars and was able to locate Polaris, which pointed due North. When they had been apprehended, they had been traveling in a Northwesterly direction, so with their eyes on Polaris they continued that way.

But, how far they had been taken off their trail by Jed and Jimbo, they had no idea. They felt that they would recognize the right road when they got to it, so they continued on, hoping that their route would take them toward Ninety-Six.

Breaking out of the woods a short time later, they realized that they had been traveling in the right direction because they came upon the road that they had been on earlier. "Hooray!" They whispered to each other, still not sure if they had been followed or not.

"Let's get this message delivered!" Will said. "We don't know if General Marion has beaten us there, so we need to get a hurry-on."

Chapter 28

By the time dawn approached, the two boys were nearly at their destination. They could see the outlying pickets guarding General Greene's command. Racing their mounts the last few yards, they were hailed by the pickets to stop where they were. Thomas called out, "We are here with a message for General Greene from General Marion. Let the general know we are here. Tell him that it is Thomas and Will. He knows us! And can you please hurry? The message is long overdue!"

Running off to alert Greene that the boys were there to see him, the guard hastily called out, "General Greene! General Greene! There are two riders here who say they have a message for you. Their names are Thomas and Will. Do you want to see them?"

"By all means, send them in!" The general shouted. The general quickly put on his coat and left his tent to wait for the boys to be ushered into his presence. "Well, lads! It's good to see you," he greeted them. "What news do you have for me? I hope that it's good because we need something to uplift our spirits!"

Thomas withdrew the message from the hidden part of his hat and handed it to the general. With a Cheshire smile, the general read the message. He was elated to learn that Georgetown had been surrendered to the Americans with all of its supplies. "Just the news I needed to hear!" He said. "Okay, boys. I need you to deliver a message back to Marion but I want you to get some rest first, and then come to see me at my tent."

The boys willingly did so. They were anxious to rest up because they had not gotten much sleep the two nights before. After eating and napping for a couple of hours, the boys found themselves in front of General Greene again. "Here is your letter, men," he said to them. "Make sure that Marion gets this message as soon as you can. I want him to go to Moncks Corner and work with Sumter to keep the British from that area. I understand that there are two thousand British soldiers in Charleston that are ready to march here. Marion needs to help Sumter stall the British progress toward Ninety-Six!"

"Yes, Sir!" They replied.

"We will be on our way in the next few minutes. Hopefully, we can intercept General Marion before he gets much farther away from Colonel Sumter."

"Good lads! Off you go, then!" Greene said.

Will and Thomas took off, headed to where they thought General Marion would be at this point in time. The only thing they knew was that Marion was headed toward Ninety-Six where he hoped to join up with Greene. Now, those plans had changed. Greene had laid siege to Ninety-Six, and was hoping to make the British surrender. But now, with those two thousand British troops on the way, his siege might not work in time.

Greene had tried several ways to overcome the Loyalist defenses at Ninety-Six to no avail. That is why he needed Marion and Sumter to do everything possible to slow down the British advance under the leadership of Lord Rawdon. Things did not go the way Greene anticipated. Will and Thomas had been successful in delivering his letter to Marion, and Marion had sent a return letter letting the General know that he was on his way to join Sumter.

Marion feared, however, that the enemy would destroy all the provisions for Greene's army if he left the area. He wanted to keep the enemy hemmed in close to Charleston and prevent them from foraging in the countryside.

After sending the last missive to Greene, Marion called his men together, "Men," he said, "General Greene wants us to help Colonel Sumter keep the British from assisting the Loyalists at Ninety-Six."

"But, General!" They cried. "That is such a far distance from our homes and families. And didn't you say that there was a two-thousand-man enemy force on the way there that we would probably encounter? Some of the militia have returned to their homes, and there are only about three hundred of us left! How can we do battle with such a small number of men? We say that we will fight when we are ready to fight! And until that time, we will stay close to home, Sir!"

Thomas and Will were surprised to hear the men sound off that way. The militia had always done what General Marion commanded, but in this case, they refused to abide by Greene's orders.

"What will we do now, General?" Thomas asked. "Will we stay here, or will we go to Ninety-Six as General Greene has requested?"

"We will wait because General Greene will be sending another order soon, I am sure," answered Marion. A few days later, General Greene did send another message. He explained that when Rawdon reached Ninety-Six with his large force, Greene felt that retreating quietly from the siege of Ninety-Six was his best option, since his five hundred men would not do well against two thousand. Lord Rawdon, himself, actually ordered the garrison to be demolished and abandoned as it no longer had enough supplies for the British army. It just wasn't worth defending anymore.

So, in the end, the loss of a battle at Ninety-Six was really a win for the Americans. This garrison had been the last major British stronghold in this part of South Carolina, and now it was gone.

There was joy in the camp when news came of its destruction, even though they weren't the ones responsible for it. However, that joy would not last because the message also sent direct orders for Marion and his militia to assist General Greene at Eutaw Springs, where they would engage a large British army under the leadership of Colonel Stewart. Arriving with his militia, Greene gave him orders to wait for his signal, and he and his men would join the fight.

As they had their own horses, Thomas and Will were waiting with the cavalry. Will looked at Thomas and wiped the sweat from his forehead. They were frightened because they had not fought in such an important battle so far against so many British. Thomas said, "Whatever happens, Will, know that you have been a great friend to me. I hope that we both get out of this battle safely."

"That's my prayer, too," said Will. "I'll watch your back. You watch mine, okay?"

Just as Thomas was about to answer, General Marion received the signal to attack. "Here we go!" Thomas yelled. "Take care, my friend! I'll see you after this battle is over!"

Racing their horses along with the others, the boys aimed their muskets at the enemy. There were so many close calls. Will almost received a bullet in the chest but Thomas's gun was aimed at the dragoon, and down he went. Will saluted his thanks to Thomas and off they tore into the fight, again. Two hours later, many dead and wounded from both sides lay in the fields but Will and Thomas were not a part of those.

Except for torn shirts and a bloody arm or leg, both lads made it safely through the worst of it. They greeted each other happily when Marion called his men together.

"We've successfully done what General Greene asked us to do this day, men. We drove their skirmishing parties back through the woods and then hit their line. I am proud of you all! You advanced steadily and unfalteringly during the enemy's hottest fire. Now, we have been given leave to take our weary horses, wounded, and dead away from here to a place where we can rest. We are heading to Caney Plantation where we have rested before."

"After we are encamped, I will dismiss those of you who have homes nearby. You behaved gallantly today." Looking at Thomas and Will, he saluted them for their own bravery during the battle.

Having dismissed the majority of his men the next day, Marion was astounded to receive another message from General Greene. In his message, Greene stated that rain had kept them from continuing the battle the following day, and Colonel Stewart had buried his dead, destroyed his supplies, left seventy wounded behind, and retreated toward Moncks Corner with the remnants of his force. Green said that he also was retreating with all of his wounded but had left a cavalry picket to cover their own orderly retreat. The picket would also ensure that a possible British advance would be stopped.

General Greene's message again ordered Marion and his tired brigade to head to another place, this one called Moncks Corner. There, they were to meet up with Colonel Lee and try to keep Stewart's British troops from retreating to Charleston. However, there's a real problem. Marion doesn't have much of a brigade left, since he had given the majority permission to go home for the time being.

The Patriots had been driven out of Moncks Corner by British troops in the spring of 1780, and now was one of only two important British outposts, besides Charleston, left in South Carolina. While General Marion was anxious to get back to this area as that was his childhood home, he needed to get his men back together again. Instead, he was stuck here at his headquarters waiting for all of his men to reassemble. He sent Simon back to General Greene to let him know that he would be there to assist Colonel Lee as soon as his men returned.

Thomas and Will were chomping at the bit. They wanted to get this war over with and were willing to do anything Marion needed to finish their goal. On the off chance that they might be able to get a head start on this mission, both young men hailed General Marion as he was strolling around the encampment, probably recounting his men to see if he had enough to continue on to Moncks Corner. Hearing the boys call out to him, he stopped mid-stride to see what they wanted from him.

"General Marion," Thomas called. "Will and I would like to help you. We know that you are as anxious to get to Moncks Corner as we are. Could we go on ahead and be your eyes and ears as we have done in the past? We know that the British are on their last legs in South Carolina, and the sooner we can oust them altogether, we can help finish this whole campaign against them and send them scurrying back to England."

Marion smiled at the two Patriotic young men and then he told them that he would give a thought to their request. He sent them on their way and hurried back to his quarters to mull over the idea. What help could they give him while he was waiting for his full detachment to be formed? He didn't know how soon they would all be available as Colonel Horry and Major James had not yet returned from recruiting more men.

As Marion sat thinking, he realized that General Greene had not given him any information about how many British troops were going to be at Monck's Corner. This was information that he felt was needed if there was going to be a successful mission. So, this was where his two young men could help. Spy out the area for him! Getting his thoughts in order, he called the sergeant outside of his tent. "Sergeant, please bring Thomas and Will to me."

"Yes, Sir," replied the sergeant as he rushed off to find Will and Thomas, who were not that far away.

"Are you looking for us, Sergeant?" Will asked. "What do you need?"

"The general wants you! Hurry! He seems to be excited about something!"

"Okay. We are on our way," answered Thomas. The two boys were trembling with excitement. Did the general have a job for them to do?

"Enter," called Marion when they knocked on the door of the tent. "Come in, men. I have decided that there is something you can do for me but I'm not sure if I should send you. I need to know how many British soldiers are guarding Moncks Corner and what's going on there. Do you think that you could sneak into Moncks Corner and gather that information? It could be very dangerous, and if you're caught as spies, the British will hang you, regardless of your age."

Will and Thomas stared at each other, their faces grim. Of all the jobs that the general could have given them, this was the worst. But knowing that this was important to the mission and to the general, they didn't hesitate in their response. "We can do it, Sir. Just tell us where you want us to go and tell us what to do!"

"Good! Here's what I need you to do. General Greene didn't tell me how many soldiers we would be encountering at Moncks Corner, so it is necessary that I have that knowledge. Do you two think that you could get close enough or even sneak into Moncks Corner to get that vital information? I'm counting on you fellows to help me out here. This information will be invaluable. Why don't you take a little time to discuss this mission with each other and let me know as soon as possible what you have decided? You're dismissed."

The boys saluted the general and then left.

"Wow!" The boys said, right after they were dismissed from the general's quarters. "He actually wants us to go right into the enemy's nest!"

"That frightens me somewhat," said Thomas. "Even after all of our encounters with the British soldiers during this war, I don't think I have been this scared! Do you have any suggestions as to what we should do to accomplish this mission, Will? I'm all out of ideas at this point. My whole body is trembling just thinking about what might happen to us if we get caught."

"I'm petrified, too," said Will, but I think we can do this.

"Moncks Corner is awfully close to Charleston!" Thomas exclaimed. "There are hundreds of British soldiers located in and around the city. We could never get close enough to Moncks Corner to spy out the numbers of dragoons posted there!"

"Hold on, Thomas! I think that I might have an idea. What if we entered Moncks Corner not as spies but as Tory lads working on the British supply lines? You know that supplies are always being delivered to the soldiers on a regular basis if possible. We could ask to join a group of suppliers on their way to Moncks Corner. They would never suspect two 'boys' to be part of Marion's militia. They would just think we wanted to help get this war over with and helping the British to do it would be a good 'in' for us. What do you think?"

"I like that idea better than trying to infiltrate their garrison to find out information," said Thomas. "Let's take your plan to the general and see if he thinks there is any merit to it."

"Okay, Thomas. I like that idea. Let's go see our commander," responded Will.

On the way to Marion's quarters, the boys discussed ways that they could become members of a supply train to the British. Hoping that General Marion liked their ideas, they knocked on his tent.

Opening the flap, Marion invited the boys in. "Well, lads. Have you come to a decision that will help me know how many soldiers we will be up against?"

"We have, Sir," they both answered and immediately went into their plan. Marion's eyebrows drew together as he listened to what they wanted to do. He wasn't sure that this idea would work as knowledge of British supplies was not bandied about in the open where the enemy could learn of it.

So he interrupted their line of thought by throwing out a question. "How will you be able to find a supply train for the British strongholds? That is information that is kept close to those only in the know. We don't let our left hand know what the right hand is doing, so I imagine that the British are doing the same."

"I have actually thought of that, Sir," Will said. "You already know that my father is in tight with Cornwallis, being a loyal Tory! Well, you also probably remember that he was ill-treated by a brigade of British soldiers who had left him for dead. That has left a bad taste in his mouth for the British powers, but from what I have heard, it has not kept him from staying on friendly terms with Cornwallis."

"Who knows, maybe it was for a time like this when we need his help. I think that he would be willing to find out that information for us. What if we were to go to the plantation and ask for his assistance?"

"That's a mighty convincing argument, Will, but are you sure that he will side with the Patriots even though that happened to him? He seems to be a pretty loyal Tory, in spite of his personal feelings."

"Well, Sir, he can only say no," responded Will. "We will make sure that he doesn't know the reason for our asking. We'll tell him that we want to join a supply train to help his cause. If he refuses because he doesn't support the British anymore, that will just be icing on the cake for us. I don't think that he would willingly put his son's life in danger, anyway. After all, I am his only heir! What do you think, General?"

"Wow! You have thought this out pretty thoroughly, Will. We really need that information, so I guess you two had better get on your horses and head out to your plantation, Will. Go with my blessing, but please, be careful! More than likely, there will be British somewhere on the plantation, either protecting him or keeping him from helping us." Marion smiled at the boys and hurried them on their way.

Chapter 29

Hastily, Will and Thomas got their gear together. Even though they were still on Snow Island, they were farther away from the plantation than they were before the older campground was destroyed. They were now several hours away from Will's home and would have to hurry to get there, talk to his father, and then return to Marion. Hopefully, Mr. Francis would be willing to help them get attached to a supply train on the way to Moncks Corner.

It might be far-fetched to think this idea would work, but they had to try, not only for Marion's sake, but for the Patriots' sake as well. Fortunately, it was early in the day, and that would give them the extra time they needed.

Coming off the island at full speed, the boys headed Southwest toward the plantation, hoping against hope that Will's father was there and that he would be willing to assist them in this endeavor. The last time Will had seen his father was when they dropped him off at the British-held Camden to get his wounds attended. They both hoped that he had less respect for his British compatriots than he did earlier.

The lads made good time. They stopped every few miles to give Ebony and Saucy time to rest up. They didn't want to endanger their horses, even though time was of the essence. Nearing mid-afternoon, they saw the gates to the plantation, and wouldn't you know it, there were British soldiers guarding the entrance. What was going on?

"Halt!" One of the guards yelled. "Who are you and what are you doing here?" Fortunately, the young men had removed their feathers from their caps, so no one would be the wiser of their affiliation with Francis Marion. To the soldiers, they looked like two British young men, even if their clothing was not what Will would normally be wearing had he been living at home.

Will took off his cap and wiped his forehead. "I live here," he responded haughtily, "and may I ask you the same question? What are you doing here? Why are you halting people from entering my father's gates? I have not been home for a couple of months as I have been visiting my friend, Thomas, here. But you haven't answered my question yet. What are you doing here?"

"We are here under General Cornwallis's orders. It seems that your father has been having some problems with interlopers and we are just helping out. We are sorry about stopping you, Sir, but we did not know that you were his son. You may continue on in, and good day to you, Sir."

"Whew!" Will said, once they were farther down the road. "I was a little surprised by that incident. I wonder what has been happening here in my absence. Now, I'm really anxious to see my father, mother, and my sisters!" They continued on down the long driveway until they finally reached the plantation. Everything seemed calm, but calmness does not always offer peace and contentment. They dismounted, tying their horses to the rail, and ran up the stairs.

No knocking on his own door, Thomas rushed in, calling for his father. He could hear shuffling in the hallway, and soon a head popped out of the library door. No! Not another soldier! Something was not right!

"Hey!" Will called out. "Who are you and what are you doing in my father's library? Nosing around where you don't belong? Where is my father?"

"Right here, son." Will turned around to see his father standing behind him. "I am so glad to see you. I hadn't heard from you in a long while and was worried that something drastic had happened to you. These men are here protecting me from some kind of foul play they think is going on around the plantation. What brings you home? Have you finally given up your other silly interests and come back to stay as the heir to this place?"

Lifting his hands, in appeal, his father raised his eyebrows at Will, as if to say, 'Please agree with me'. Will caught the anxious look in the eyes of his father and immediately understood that something was amiss!

"Uh, yes, Father, and I have brought Thomas back with me. You had said that you wanted to meet him the last time we talked. Together, we have decided to come back and help you run this plantation. But tell me why you need protection, Father. We have seen no indication of trouble going on or brewing around this area. Why are these soldiers here?"

"It's a long story, Will." Putting his arm around Will's shoulder, Mr. Francis said, "Let's take a walk outside and you can tell me what you have been doing in the last couple of months." His father seemed in no hurry to get outside, so maybe nothing was amiss after all. Will and Thomas both relaxed as they headed outside into the warmth of the afternoon. Picking up the conversation, again, Mr. Francis continued, "Remember the day you lads saved my life? Well, those men were brought to justice and drummed out of His Majesty's army."

"However, they threatened our family because I had told General Cornwallis about the incident that got them kicked out. Cornwallis has been very cognizant of the fact that I might be persuaded to join the Patriot side because of those soldiers, so he has stationed soldiers here to keep an eye on me—he said to protect me, but I think it is his way of spying on me so that I don't use any opportunity to help his enemies."

He sighed, then tried to smile, but Will and Thomas knew that this was hard on him, a man who had always been loyal to the Crown. "So, Will, what has kept you away from home for so long?"

Will gulped. He didn't know what to tell his father, so he asked him a question instead. "How loyal are you to the Crown, Father? Do you still side with them? You know that's why I left the plantation. I couldn't abide the slaughter of innocents and destruction of land and property by the so-called superior soldiers of the British military. I know that has happened on both sides but I feel that there is more compassion on the side of the Patriots."

"To answer your question, Will, I have thought long and hard about which side I am truly on. There are pros and cons for each, but after the incident with the British soldiers, who would actually treat a loyal Tory like myself unkindly, I have my own questions. I do think that the Patriots have a just cause for rebelling against the mother country, even though it hurts me to say it. If push comes to shove, I think that I might well become a Patriot, especially now, with all of these British soldiers keeping an eye on the family."

"Your mother and sisters have been allowed to leave the plantation to visit friends and family not far from here, but they were sent with a troop of soldiers to keep an eye on them. I am really under house arrest until I am proven innocent of harboring and aiding the enemy. I have unburdened my heart to you, Will. Now tell me, in what kind of trouble have you been engaging?"

Now, the truth had to come out. His father had been honest with him, so how could he not reciprocate? Thomas cleared his throat and gave Will the heads up to go ahead with the reason they were here. "Well, Father, while you have been supporting the British, I have been supporting the Patriots. Thomas and I are a part of Francis Marion's brigade. I pray that you will not deliver us into the hands of Cornwallis because that would mean our deaths."

"We are here on a mission from General Marion. We need your help. Marion wants us to infiltrate Moncks Corner to find out how many soldiers he will be up against in a few days. We were hoping to pretend to be on the side of the British and gain entry to the fortification as helpers in delivering supplies to the soldiers there. Is there a way you can help us? If not, then let us please leave without alerting the soldiers that are here."

Chapter 30

Mr. Francis looked thoughtfully at the two young men. He had never imagined for a moment that when Will left he would be so brave as to take part in the war, especially on the opposite side of his father and other members of the family! Unbelievable! Now, it would be his turn to do the surprising and he stood quietly wondering how he could tell Will and Thomas everything that had transpired since he last saw them.

Giving a loud harrumph, as if trying to remove the gruffness of his throat, he stared pointedly at the boys, who were now standing with nervous twitches, waiting for his reaction to their news. He was about to relieve them of their nervousness! "Well, Will and Thomas, the last time you saw me was under very trying circumstances. You dropped me off at a British fortification for my physical health, but while there, my mental health increased as well."

"What I am saying is this. I have turned to the Patriot side of the cause. Here is the reason why. After my ordeal, I went to General Cornwallis's headquarters and complained about the treatment meted out to me by his brigade of soldiers, almost killing me and my driver, Joe."

Pausing, Mr. Francis pulled his tricorn off his head and scratched behind his ear, not sure how to continue with his story, without making General Cornwallis look so bad in the eyes of the two boys, for he was still a Britisher at heart, even if he now disagreed with the leadership. "Anyway, when I told him what happened, he started laughing! Can you imagine that? Just stood there laughing at the incident. He tried to make it look like just a prank on the part of his soldiers. I couldn't believe it!"

"We could have died out there waiting for help! When I expressed my displeasure to him, he promised to chastise the soldiers and give them less pay in their next packet. Later, I heard that all he had done was to give them a slight slap on the wrists, as if they had done nothing wrong! So, yes, son! In answer to your question, I will help you. It's the least I can do for the cause."

"I am so relieved to hear you say that, Father!" Will exclaimed. "We didn't know what we would do if we couldn't count on your help. The first question is this. Do you happen to know how many soldiers Cornwallis has at his command for his next attack? Secondly, do you know where he might be heading in the next few days? And most importantly, how can we get off the plantation with British guards all around us?"

"We could be in a tight pickle here, if you know what I mean. General Marion is expecting us back with information as soon as possible. He had expected us to infiltrate Moncks Corner as part of a British supply company, but if you have the information already, we won't have to make that trip. Especially considering the fact that we could be hung if caught spying!"

"What? You were going to Moncks Corner as spies? Incredible! What would make you do such a dangerous thing? I understand your commitment to the Patriot cause, but this is going way beyond loyalty. This is foolishness! I am proud of your bravery but, Will, you are my only son, and look at you, Thomas. You are only fifteen years old and you would risk your life, too?"

"I appreciate the kind of men that this war is turning you and others into but I can't allow you to go on this dangerous journey. First, let me find out what I can from the captain who is staying in our house and then I will help you escape from here after I get what information I can. In the meantime, just hang around the house listening and gaining as much information as you can. Just act like you are young men without a care in the world." Saying that, Mr. Francis raised his hands and walked away as if he had grown tired of talking to the two upstart young men.

The boys mosied on back toward the entrance of the manor house, looking around and discussing anything that came into their heads. They needed to keep these guards unaware of what they were up to. It was necessary that they let the guards see them often enough that they would not become suspicious of the two young men. Just act normal, Mr. Francis said, and that's what they would do, keeping their ears and eyes open at all times.

While the boys were wandering around, Mr. Francis hustled into the house looking for Captain Hunt. He knew that the captain would be full of information and so Francis had kept close to him since the soldier's arrival at his plantation. He knew when and where the captain would be discussing missions and issues with his underlings, so he hurried to his own bedroom above the library. Fortunately, the soldiers had allowed Mrs. Francis and his daughters to take a short carriage ride to the next plantation to visit their neighbors, so he had the house to himself, aside from the soldiers, that was.

Many of the plantation homes had been built so that heat and cool air could travel upward through the ceiling to keep the rooms warmer in the colder seasons and cooler in the hotter times of the year. It was to one of these vents that Mr. Francis hurried. Quietly kneeling down so that he could put his ear to the vent, he listened to what was going on in the library. Sure enough, the captain was in there talking to his sergeant and aide.

Captain Hunt told the men, "I have received a message from General Cornwallis telling me that we should hold our positions here until he notifies us to do otherwise. He is still unsure if Mr. Francis is on our side or on the side of the Patriots."

Continuing, Hunt said, "He has informed me that his forces are large enough to withstand any attacks on Moncks Corner, and that he expects a raid by the Swamp Fox and the rest of the Continentals soon. He is fairly confident that such an attack will not be successful. He is determined to keep South Carolina in our hands and not let it be taken by those homespun rebels!"

"Sergeant, you are dismissed to go about your duties, keeping your eyes on Mr. Francis and now those two boys who have recently arrived. I am not sure that I trust any of them." Speaking to his aide, George, he said, "I must send a note to General Cornwallis to let him know I have received his message and will plan to stay here at Francis Hall until I am needed elsewhere."

Silently, Mr. Francis withdrew from the vent and considered what he had heard. He knew that this would be information that General Marion would need, so he nonchalantly walked down the stairs and out the front door. Nodding to the soldier on duty, he told him that he was going to take a walk in the gardens and get some fresh air. The soldier nodded his understanding and stood guard at his post, allowing Mr. Francis to wander to the gardens alone.

"Will! Thomas! Come here!" He shouted in a loud enough voice that the soldiers could hear him and not be suspicious of his activity. He noticed two soldiers grinning because they thought Will and Thomas were going to be in trouble. Great! That's just what he wanted as he waited by the sundial in the garden.

Will and Thomas slowly approached him and slung themselves down on the bench in a sullen attitude, just as Mr. Francis expected them to do. He needed to look like he was chastising them for something that they apparently did which was not to his liking. Raising his voice, he started to harangue them for being worthless young men, not helping their mother country to win this war.

"What's wrong with you, anyway? Other young men your age are already in the army but here you sit doing nothing! I am ashamed of you both," he said. "With Captain Hunt's permission, tomorrow, I am tossing you off this property. Don't return until you have proven that you are loyal to the Crown." Under his breath, he whispered, "I think I have the information you are looking for. Come to my bedroom after dinner and I will tell you then. Captain Hunt should not grow suspicious when a son goes to his father's bedroom to say his goodbyes!"

Bowing their heads, as if in a sense of shame, the two boys nodded. "Yes, Father."

Will said loudly in a tearful voice. "I am sorry that I have angered you and brought you to the point of disowning me. I hope to return and get your blessing soon." So saying, Will and Thomas slowly slumped away with downtrodden shoulders.

That evening, after having dinner with Captain Hunt and Mr. Francis, the two young men made their excuses to leave the table. They said that since they were being forced to leave the plantation, they needed to get their things together for the morrow. They paid their respects to the captain and told Mr. Francis that they would come to his bedroom later to bid him goodbye, for, with Captain Hunt's permission, they would leave in the early morning.

They slowly left the dining room as if they had been totally dejected. On their way up the stairs to Will's room, the boys paused to listen to anything that Captain Hunt would say to Mr. Francis.

"Well, Francis, it seems that you are rather disappointed in your son, Will. What has he done to make you treat him in such a fashion? He seemed like a nice young man to me."

"Unfortunately, Captain, it's not what he has done but what he hasn't done. Being my only son, he has been spoiled all of his life and has lived like nothing in the world should concern him. I told him in no uncertain terms that if he didn't start acting like a man, I would disown him. He needs to keep in mind that he is a British citizen and should act accordingly. That means joining up to fight for the Crown and not hanging out with those who would dissuade him from doing that."

"Thomas is a good young man but his life is also one of dissolution. Both boys need to get it all together. So, I have sent Will off, so that he can decide whether he wants to still be part of this family by doing the right thing." Mr. Francis shrugged his shoulders in abject defeat as if he really was sorry about his son's lack of action.

Taking a sip of his tea, the father continued, "So, Captain Hunt, if you would permit the boys to leave in the morning, I would sincerely appreciate it. He needs to learn that I mean business!"

"If that's your desire, Sir. Of course, I will let them depart, with a warning that they should not return until they are wearing the King's colors. How does that suit you?"

"Thank you, Captain," gushed Mr. Francis. "I will inform the boys of what you have ordered when they come to my room tonight. Now, I'm tired. I pray that you will forgive my leaving the table so early. All of this has taken a toll on me and I am ready to rest for the night. At least, I will, as soon as I have said goodbye to my son and Thomas. Please excuse me!"

Captain Hunt nodded his head in understanding and remained seated at the table as Mr. Francis exited the room. As soon as he finished his tea, he took his leave of the table and headed back to the library to listen in on the conversation that would soon take place in Mr. Francis's suite.

Thomas and Will hustled up the stairs to pack their belongings and waited until Mr. Francis strode past their door before they followed him to his bedroom. Will knocked on his father's door. "Come in," his father responded. Will pushed open the door but before Will and Thomas could say anything, Mr. Francis held his index finger to his lips, letting them know that they should remain quiet. He held a piece of paper out to them with the words 'Don't speak! I'm sure that the captain is in the library listening to whatever we say here!'. The boys nodded their understanding.

"Well, Will and Thomas, I am sorry that this situation has come to pass. I had hoped, Will, that you would join the British grenadiers but you haven't, and I cannot allow you to remain on the plantation until you come about to my way of thinking!" As Will's father said those words, he held out a piece of paper with the information that General Marion needed.

Continuing, he said, "Will, I don't want to see you back here until you have decided to join me as a true Loyalist, or until this war is over. Captain Hunt is doing me a favor by allowing you to leave this plantation in the morning. Make sure you stay away from here because I have no desire to see you. You have shamed me by your careless attitude! Good night. I will not plan on seeing you again unless you are in uniform! Is that clear?"

"Yes, Father," said Will in a dejected voice. "I am sorry that I have caused you so much pain. Please give my love to mother and my sisters. Goodbye, Sir!" Slowly, the two young men left the bedroom and slouched back to Will's room to complete their packing. In case anyone was observing, they needed to make it clear that they were being tossed out, so sadness encompassed their faces, rather than the joy they were feeling on the inside.

Once they got back to the room, they quietly looked at the note. It looked like what the general was hoping to learn. They smiled at each other and then lay down on the bed to await the morning.

Chapter 31

Arising very early the next morning, Will and Thomas took their leave of the plantation. The guards at the entrance allowed them to pass without anyone questioning them. Captain Hunt must have given notice to the soldiers that they should not interfere but let the two young men pass without any problems. He felt that they would return soon enough wearing British colors. Little did he know that he was actually helping the Swamp Fox by allowing those two young men to escape his clutches.

As soon as they were out of sight of the plantation, Will and Thomas kicked their horses into a steady gallop. Without speaking to one another, they flew down the trail until they were at least five miles away from the British. Slowing their horses to a lighter gait, the lads took time to discuss what had occurred with Mr. Francis. It seemed as if he had actually taken the side of the Patriots. Otherwise, why would he have helped them?

Will spoke, "Thomas, do you think my father actually has switched sides? I know him and that seems to be an unusual stance for him to take. Once his mind is set to something, he is hardly ever dissuaded! I am just so surprised that he was willing to help us, and I am now worried that he will get in trouble with the British who are at the plantation, containing him like a prisoner in his own house."

"Do you think that the information he gave us is true, or was he just trying to give General Marion false information? I am in a dither over it all."

Thomas responded, "Will, I think that your father was sincere. I feel that he has really turned a corner and is now on our side. His earlier incident with Cornwallis's soldiers have soured him to the cause of the Crown. I wouldn't be surprised if he decided to join us and General Marion. He seemed impressed with our commander."

As they continued on, both boys kept their thoughts to themselves as they contemplated their time at the plantation. They both knew that the British were suspicious of Mr. Francis, else why would there be soldiers stationed in his home? The very fact that Captain Hunt listened in on their conversation in the bedroom told them that Mr. Francis was really under house arrest. Now, what could they do to free him?

Will began speaking again. "Thomas, how can we free my father from those soldiers? I don't want anything to happen to him. I am so glad that my mother and my sisters are at my aunt's home. It would be terrible for them to be at the mercy of those soldiers!"

"I was just thinking the very same thing," Thomas said. "When we get back to the island, let's talk to the general about it and see what suggestions he might make in order to help your father break off those chains that are holding him there. Surely, he will be able to think of something. But first, we need to get this information that your father gave us to him, and time is running out fast!"

"Agreed," said Will, as he took off galloping down the road, with Thomas not far behind. If they could travel a little faster without wearing out their horses, they could make good time and, possibly, they might be able to make it back to the island by nightfall. With that goal in mind, the boys kept up their speed, stopping occasionally to give their mounts time to rest. Since they had left very early in the morning, they still had almost a full day before dark befell them.

Just before sunset, the boys barreled into camp. The guard had been alerted and had given permission to enter. Hailing Simon, they passed the reins of their horses over to him, and sped toward General Marion's quarters. He had already been told that the boys were back, and so he stepped out as soon as he heard the horses ride into camp. "Well, lads, I'm glad to see you back in one piece. I was concerned when we didn't hear anything from you. We thought that you had been captured or something worse had happened. But, I see that you are both fit. Come into my quarters and tell me all about your trip."

"Yes, Sir," Will and Thomas answered. They were itching to tell their general everything.

Thomas started the conversation. "Well, Sir, you sent us on a mission to find out as much as we could about the condition of General Cornwallis's troops and how many he had to hold Moncks Corner. You know that we planned to be a part of a supply train taking materials to his soldiers. Well, when we got to Will's home, our plans changed. For the better, I might add. Will, you tell the general what transpired on your plantation since it's your home."

"Okay," said Will. "Imagine our surprise, Sir, when we arrived at my home to find British soldiers guarding the gates and the whole plantation! We couldn't figure out what was going on. I told the guard at the gate that I was Will Francis, the son of the plantation owner, and that my friend, Thomas, and I were returning from seeing other friends elsewhere. The guard let us through and as we looked around, there were soldiers everywhere with their guns on their shoulders, as if they were planning on being attacked."

"We raced up the front steps to the door and entered the house, only to see my father coming from the library with Captain Hunt right behind him. My father must have noticed the quizzical look on my face, so he quickly introduced us to the captain and explained why the soldiers were quartered in our house. Supposedly, they were there to protect him but he didn't say who he was supposed to be protected from."

At this point, Thomas jumped into the explanation. "After a little while, Mr. Francis asked us to walk in the garden with him. He said that although he and General Cornwallis were on the best of terms, the general had sent these soldiers to watch over him for some reason. He believed that Cornwallis didn't trust him now because of what had happened to Mr. Francis when he was almost killed by Cornwallis's soldiers. Well, Mr. Francis asked us what we were doing at the plantation. We didn't want to lie to Will's father and, because we didn't know what to say, Will just blurted out the truth, Sir."

Marion's eyebrows rose at that admission, and Thomas assured him that all was well because Mr. Francis had already changed his allegiance. He was now on the side of the Patriots!

"So, lads. Were you able to acquire the information that I needed? Obviously, you didn't have to masquerade as British Loyalists to get into Moncks Corner, otherwise you wouldn't be back so soon! So, Mr. Francis must have helped you. What did he tell you?" He asked a little impatiently.

"That's what's so good, Sir," answered Will. "He was able to listen in on a conversation between the British captain and his sergeant-major. He discovered that the British are planning on retreating to Charleston, and if you want to keep them from arriving there, my father suggested that you leave as soon as possible."

"You're sure that your father is on the side of the Patriots, Will? He won't be planning on having us ambushed, will he?" Marion asked.

"Oh no, Sir! My father is on the up-and-up. He would never betray me or double-cross you. He knows that you know where he lives," added Will.

"All right! Sergeant, gather the men. We have a job to finish. We need to meet up with Colonel Lee and keep those Redcoats from returning to Charleston!" With that, Marion prepared to go to battle a second time in two days with a militia that was still exhausted and recovering from the last battle.

As he was giving directions, Simon returned from his trip delivering Marion's previous letter to General Greene. "General Marion!" He called. "I have delivered your message to the general and he wants you to hasten to Colonel Lee's side as soon as you can get the men together. He said to tell you that he received word that Stewart is already getting his force together and getting ready to leave for Charleston. He wants you and Colonel Lee to get in between the two British forces, and keep them from putting a much stronger army together, and he said that you need to move fast!"

*****

In the meantime, thinking that the Continentals and militia would attack again, Stewart sent a message to Major McArthur to bring his dragoons to help in case the rebels wanted to take another shot at them.

*****

While Stewart was sending his letter to McArthur, General Marion had his men form their ranks and prepare to move out to assist Colonel Lee at Moncks Corner. Thomas and Will queued up in the line at the end of the cavalry, hoping to support the militia wherever they were needed. As soon as Marion and his men met up with Lee, both men led their forces swiftly through the night, but not fast enough, for unfortunately, Stewart and McArthur had already joined their forces and had continued their trek back to Charleston.

Lee and Marion decided that there was no need to put their soldiers in harm's way by charging into a larger army, so retired to their own encampments for the time being until General Greene needed them again. Will and Thomas heaved a great sigh of relief. They were tired and had not cherished facing the enemy again so soon.

Marion led his militia across the Santee River again and encamped on familiar territory near the Caney Plantation, where they knew that they would be safe from any Britishers. He dismissed his men and told them to get their rest. There would be no telling when Greene would want them back in the fight. Will and Thomas were ready to make their beds and get some well-earned rest as well.

Chapter 32

After receiving their much-needed rest, the militia was on the move again. Greene had requested that Marion and his militia expend their efforts to drive all the British into Charleston, where they could be contained by the Continentals. Then rumors drifted into Marion's camp that there had been skirmishes between Loyalists and Patriots.

While they were resting up, Thomas said, "I'm just about ready for this war to end! What do you think, Will? Are you ready to go back to help your father at the plantation and further your education? Are you as tired as I am? I have enjoyed getting to know all the men and General Marion but enough's enough!"

"You sound like you would like to quit right now," stated Will as he continued to whittle the wood in his hand. He obviously was still thinking about how to answer Thomas. He ached to know what was going on at his plantation and how his family was doing. Yet, he knew this war was not going to be over as soon as he would have liked. Looking at Thomas, he laid aside his knife and wood and nodded his head in agreement.

Interrupting Will before he said anything else, Thomas remonstrated, "I am not ready to quit, Will. I will stay as long as General Marion and the militia need me. But I would like to go home, sooner rather than later!"

"I understand, Thomas. I feel the same way. We have had our fair share of adventures, but like you, I am ready to go home. If it weren't for General Marion and his need for all of us, I would be headed there right now. I know that our commander is also getting tired of the non-stop ambushes, the lack of rest, and all of the killing. We both heard the news from that Whig spy that the Carolina Loyalists had suffered greatly and that the British power was steadily deteriorating."

"However, the latest news is that in an act of desperation, the Tories captured the governor and made him a prisoner. Their bravado aroused other Tories to pick up arms again and they have caused much mayhem around the area. So, I think that, at this point, we will be in the thick of it again. I am sure General Marion will be expecting another dispatch soon."

Indeed, Will was right. The Swamp Fox received an assignment but not from Greene this time. Governors Martin and Mathews asked Marion to lead his militia and those in the surrounding area to chase down some British that were still lingering close by and causing mayhem. As Marion digested the contents of the letter, he called Colonel Horry and Major James to his quarters.

When they arrived, he announced, "The governors are having trouble with some of the Tories in the area and he wants me to lead a charge to clear them out of the Carolinas. We need to get as many men as we can back into camp, so that I can follow through on those orders. Can I put you both in charge of rustling up as many of our militia as you can?"

"Yes, Sir!" The two men responded. Leaving the general's quarters, they hustled to their separate areas to round up the fighting men. As the members of the militia scurried about collecting gear and horses, Major James and Colonel Horry ordered their aides to round up the rest of the men who had gone home to take care of their families while waiting for their next assignment.

"Here we go again," exclaimed Thomas to Will that same afternoon. "It looks like we're on the move! Just like we thought. No rest for the weary, Will!"

"Well, we are at war, Thomas! And until this is all over, we won't get much rest. Let's get our gear together because the general will be calling us all out sooner than we think."

"I'm right behind you, Will. No sense in complaining or lollygagging around. Let's get these British soldiers out of our hair, once and for all!"

"Okay. I'm all for that," replied Will.

As the two boys were gearing up, several of the militia arrived back at the camp, having been warned by the major and colonel that they would be moving out against the British very soon. The whole camp was in a hubbub! Clearly, every time they thought that they were cleared of the British, more would pop up out of nowhere, and it was time that the foolishness ended as far as General Marion and his men were concerned. Now, they were charged, again, with routing out more British stragglers who were up to no good.

For a few weeks now, General Marion had been fighting a cold and pesky flu symptoms, and he was anxious to get back to his own bed on his own plantation. His trusty vinegar and water didn't seem to be helping him now. However, he knew that more work had to be done before that would be happening, so he called his men together and prepared to march them toward the Tories who were causing the turmoil.

He called out to the two lads, "Thomas and Will! Come to the front of the line with me. I need to discuss something with you."

"Yes, Sir!" The boys responded. They prodded their horses to do the general's bidding.

"While we are rousting out those Tories, I want you to deliver a message to General Greene. I am sure that he doesn't know what the governors have asked of me, so I would like you to find him and tell him what the militia is up to. Can you do that quickly?"

"We'll try, Sir," said Thomas. "But do you know where he is?"

Marion took off his helmet and scratched his head. "Well, the last time I heard from him he was making his way to Charleston to finish chasing the Redcoats out of the Carolinas. I would head in that direction first but be careful, there is still danger out there!"

"Yes, Sir," responded the two young men. "We'll find General Greene as soon as we can and let him know that you were called out by the governors of the two states." Thus said, they turned their horses and headed in the direction of Charleston, hoping to catch the General before it got much later in the day, because they wanted to be back at General Marion's side, routing out another group of Tories.

Urging their mounts to go faster, within two hours the boys were relieved to see the dust of General Greene's main army about one half-hour ahead. To be sure that they would not be shot at, the boys called out that they were delivering a message to the general from General Francis Marion. Fortunately, the soldiers recognized the white feathers in Thomas's and Will's caps and let them go on through, telling them that General Greene was about twenty minutes ahead of the main body.

Tipping their hats in salute, Thomas and Will decided to save time and bypass the main army by following a trail that ran beside the main road. They would cut their time in half by doing this, and would be able to reach General Greene in good time. However, they did not foresee what was ahead of them on this grassy trail. No sooner did they start galloping along the path, when Will looked at Thomas, put his index finger over his mouth, and made a sh…sh…sh sound. Then he pointed toward a place about a hundred yards ahead.

Startled, Thomas did not know why Will was being so secretive, nor did he see what Will was pointing at. Will signaled him to follow quietly. Fortunately, they had not removed the stockings from their horses' hooves, so no one had heard their approach. At least, not yet! Will backtracked on the trail and then stopped to quietly tell Thomas what he had seen.

"There are men ahead on the trail. I saw the flashes of the sun on their muskets. Could this be a part of the Tories that General Marion is supposed to find? I don't understand why they have not attacked the general and the army!"

"Maybe they don't have enough men to attack," said Thomas, "or they are waiting for backup. We didn't see how many Tories there were, so we can't just go racing in there and shooting off our guns. We will just get ourselves killed. So, what shall we do now? We have to get Marion's message to General Greene, and somehow let the General know that he and his men are about to be ambushed. What to do? What to do? Do you have any ideas, Will?"

"You've given me an idea, Thomas. It has to do with shooting off our guns! Why don't we sneak a little closer and fire toward them? When Greene hears the shooting, he will know that the enemy is close by and do the necessary thing by having his men check out the gunfire and then descend on the enemy. We just have to make sure that we are well out of the way of the army's deadly aim."

"Enough guns firing at the Tories should scare them away, with them being none the wiser that there were only two young fellows shooting at first. It will be a joke on them. As soon as they run off, we can head to General Greene and let him know that his men have scared the enemy off!"

"Do you think it will work, Will? That's a mighty long shot. What if the army has gotten farther away and won't be able to shoot back because they can't figure out where the shots came from? What if they find us before the general's men can get close enough to see the Tories? Just asking, Will. It's a good idea, and I'm with you. Let's go!"

Quietly, the boys led their horses toward the Tories. When they were within a hundred yards, they started shooting into the air and toward the hiding group. Some of their bullets must have hit their targets because several cries of woe could be heard by the boys. Their intention had not been to hurt anyone but to scare them enough to cause them to run in the opposite direction, away from the gunfire. Will and Thomas hoped that their ruse was working because they were quickly using up a lot of ammunition.

In the meantime, General Greene had heard the gunfire, and thinking that they were being fired upon, he motioned to his troops to scatter in the wooded area. He also sent two scouts to see who was shooting at them. Skirting the edges of the shooting zone, the scouts came upon Will and Thomas, hunkered down behind some bushes close to a trail that had not been noticed by Greene when he rode by earlier. The two scouts crouched down beside the boys, their eyebrows raised in question.

"What's going on? Who are you shooting at?" One of them asked. Fortunately, the men had recognized the boys from seeing them in General Greene's camp and had not shot at them.

Quickly, Will and Thomas explained what they were doing and why and that they needed to inform General Greene that there were Tories in the bushes ready to attack his men. The two men nodded, telling Will and Thomas to stay where they were, and quietly rounded up their horses. They took off in the direction of the army which was now hidden along the way.

Upon reaching the general, the two scouts told him about Will and Thomas and their ingenious decision to force the Tories to show themselves. They had to get the general's attention, somehow, and this is what they had come up with.

The general smiled and shook his head. "Those two young men have saved my men and me once again," he said. "Let's go help them out, shall we? Get the colonel and have him take some soldiers to assist Will and Thomas, and after the Tories have been scattered, bring the two young men to me."

"Yes, Sir!" The men exclaimed as they hurried to find the colonel and have him follow through with the general's orders.

Less than an hour later, the colonel returned with his men and informed the general that the terrified Tories were scattered hither and yon. "They won't be trying that trick again," said the colonel. "I guess that they will return later to collect their wounded and possible fatalities. Will and Thomas are pretty clever, Sir, even if I do say so myself!"

"Where are those two young whippersnappers?" Greene asked.

"Here we are, Sir," responded Thomas with a salute.

"Well done, men," stated the general. "You were in the right place at the right time once more," he added. "General Marion needs to promote you, even though you are only volunteers. Where is Marion, anyway?"

"That's why we are here, General Greene," replied Will. "General Marion wanted us to deliver a message that the two Carolinian governors have asked him to round up some rowdy Tories and Royalists still in the area. He had responded to their pleas before he got your last message. So, here we are, Sir, giving you that message. It was fortunate that we decided to take that trail beside the road to save time. If we hadn't, we would not have seen the Tory brigade waiting to ambush you."

"Again, I am in your debt. Please tell Marion that I understand his situation, and will wait upon his arrival at his earliest convenience. Before you leave, I insist that you rest and have a meal with us. I have ordered the men to bivouac for the night, since it is already getting close to dusk. I do not want to travel during the night in case there are more ambushes planned. So, go ahead and tell the cook to feed you. Then find a place to rest yourselves and your mounts. Just let me know before you leave camp because I want you to deliver another message to Marion."

"Yes, Sir!" The two young men said as they headed toward the cook and his helpers who were already preparing the night's meal for the men. The two boys accepted the biscuits and gravy that the cook offered to them, their noses taking in the tantalizing aroma of the meal which they were anxious to put in their growling stomachs. Sitting quickly at the base of an old oak tree, they ate their fill, washing it down with water from their canteens.

"Wow! That sure hit the spot," said Thomas. "Who knew how good such a simple meal could taste when you're close to starving!"

Laughingly, Will responded. "I guess you never know, unless you're starving, and that seems to be you all the time, Thomas. Do you ever fill up? You must have a hollow leg because you are always hungry!"

"I'm a growing boy, Will. What can I say? Do you remember how many long days we have had with little food? I can't help enjoying it when it's placed before me. I know that you enjoy eating as well as I do," Thomas joked.

"I guess that we had better finish up and get the rest that General Greene feels we need," said Will. "I think that an hour should be plenty. What do you say, Thomas?"

"An hour sounds about right for me," answered Thomas, and putting his head down on the ground, he fell fast asleep.

Will sighed, closed his eyes, and followed Thomas's example. About an hour later, he awakened with a start. It was already dark. They had slept for more than an hour it seemed. He rolled over and poked Thomas in the shoulder. "Wake up, Thomas! It's time we were on our way."

Thomas rolled over and immediately sat up. It was so quiet in the camp, he could hardly tell there was an army of men around him. But as he listened intently, he could hear the sounds of soft snoring close by. "Okay, Will. I'm awake. Let's get to General Greene's quarters and get that letter for Marion. I'm glad we hobbled our horses close by. At least we won't have to look for them among the rest of the stock. It's a good thing we took their saddles off before we ate, too. Now they will be well-rested, as well."

"We have a long ride back to Marion's headquarters before sunrise, and Ebony and Saucy will need all the stamina they can get, especially if we are met by some of those Tories and have to outrun them."

Thomas and Will hustled to get their horses saddled, so that they could be on their way. Stopping by General Greene's quarters, he wished them a safe return trip and handed them the letter he had penned for Marion. "Watch your backs, boys! Be safe, and give my regards to Marion," he said.

"Thank you, Sir! We will! You be safe, too, General." Smiling and waving at the general, they turned their horses in the direction of Marion's army.

Several long and tiring hours later, Will and Thomas finally joined up with General Marion and his militia. By this time, Marion and his men had ousted all the Tories and Loyalists in the area and had arrived back at Snow Island where they would restock their ammunition and food supplies. They, too, were weary from the day's events and were ready to bunk down for the night.

After delivering General Greene's missive to Marion, the boys headed back to their sleeping area.

Chapter 33

Early the next morning, everyone in the camp was up and about. Marion was hustling all of the militiamen to get their gear ready for the trip to join General Greene. Since the general had told the men about the beating given to the British at Saratoga, they had been rejuvenated. Now, all the talk was about how soon the war would be completely over. Everywhere Thomas and Will went, they heard conversation between the men.

Listening to one group, they heard one soldier say, "The war is about to end! We've let those British know that we mean business!" Others were saying that they could hardly wait to get home. There was an air of joy and exhilaration that spread among the men and caused them to hurry and comply with the general's orders to ready themselves. Not many grumblings and complaints could be heard this morning!

By mid-morning, the cavalry was seated on horses and the soldiers were all in line to do the general's bidding. At the head of the line, Marion sat and motioned for his officers to join him, saying, "I don't know what Greene wants us to do, or even if he will still need us when we get to the rendezvous, but in any case, be wary of who or what is surrounding you. We are still at war, even though this area of South Carolina is almost free of British troops and Tories." The men nodded their heads in agreement and then returned to their own units. Word was then passed along from the officers to the men.

Thomas and Will listened intently to Colonel Horry who was still in charge of the cavalry. He told them to remain alert and steadfast, and especially to watch their surroundings for possible ambushes. Having experienced being ambushed many times so far in this war, the two young men nodded to the colonel to let him know they understood the importance of always being vigilant. Like Thomas and Will, the other men also understood the danger that still could be near. It was necessary to be constantly attentive to any surprising sounds or things that looked out of place.

Now that they were all ready to get under way, General Marion lifted his arm and directed the men to go forward. Moving at a slower pace than normal, Marion led his militia, both cavalry and foot soldiers, along the trail leading away from their headquarters. Barely an hour out, a rider came hurrying toward Marion. All the men were immediately on the alert. What news could it be? Could the war be over? No, not yet. Everyone knew that the British were still in Charleston.

Being with General Marion for nearly two years now, Thomas never knew what to expect on a daily basis, so this message could be great news or it could be disastrous! Looking at Will, seated beside him on Saucy, he wondered aloud, "I hope this is good news, Will. There has to be a break in this war at some point."

Will nodded in agreement as they both looked toward Marion who had, by now, accepted the message from the courier. The general took the missive handed to him and slowly perused the message. After a short moment, with all eyes on him, Marion turned with a slight smile on his face. "Gather around, men, General Greene has just received and passed on some pertinent news that I'm sure you will all want to hear. It has taken a while for this information to get to us but here it is."

"From all of the information that has been supplied to us through General Greene, I know that you are aware that General Washington has been trying to outwit the British and General Cornwallis at every turn. Well, it seems that he's finally done it! General Washington was finally able to trap General Cornwallis at Yorktown, VA. On 28 September, just a few short weeks ago, the general put the city of Yorktown under siege."

"Apparently, after being outnumbered and outfought during a three-week siege which exhausted the British army's supplies of food and ammunition, and with heavy losses and no hope of escape, the British troops under Cornwallis surrendered to the Continental Army and our French allies on 19 October."

Marion's men started yelling and clapping, with Huzzahs ringing all along the trail. Everyone, including Thomas and Will were hugging, with some even having tears running down their cheeks. It seemed to the men that the end was in sight. They would soon be able to return to their homes and get on with living.

Somehow, Marion was able to get everyone's attention again. "Men, may I remind you that while this is a great win, the war is not over. There are still going to be skirmishes because the British are not going to give up yet. They have lost a major battle but they are still in control of our own seaport of

Charleston, as well as New York and Savanna. We have to continue to be vigilant. Some may even wish to do even more harm to us because of their humiliation at Yorktown.”

“We can only hope that their demoralizing loss will diminish the Britishers’ will to continue to fight us rebels. Until Charleston is completely evacuated by the British soldiers who are stationed there, South Carolina will still keep fighting.”

“What will we do now, General? Will we continue on to Charleston or stay here until we are asked to participate in another battle?” Thomas asked.

“That’s a good question, Thomas. As part of this letter, General Greene has asked that we stand down for now. While he would like to strive on to Charleston, and force those Tories, Royalists, and soldiers out, General Washington has asked that we just keep protecting this part of South Carolina. He does not expect to see much more fighting in our area. He feels that most of the pockets of resistance will continue to be groups of soldiers along with their Tory friends.”

“So, men, it looks like we can rest for a while. I suggest that those of you who can, return to your homes and families and pick up where you left off before the war. Eventually, I will return to my headquarters until I receive further orders from General Greene. Anyone who has no immediate place to go is welcome to join me there. Thank you all for your loyalty to this country. You deserve a good long break from the disasters that have befallen us lately!”

Will and Thomas looked at each other. This was certainly good news but what were they to do in the meantime? Thomas lived too far away to go home and Will wasn’t sure what had happened at his father’s plantation after they had left a few months ago.

Thomas said, “So, this is it! The war is basically over! I have made so many good friends here in the militia, I hate to see us all go our separate ways. Will, what are you going to do? Your plantation is only a few hours away, so will you head on home?”

“I don’t think so, not yet, anyway. I think that I want to stay with the general until we know for sure what is happening in the rest of the country. Won’t you stay, too, Thomas?”

“I will!” Thomas responded. “I want to see this thing through to the end. Let’s join General Marion at his headquarters. Others of his brigade will be joining him there as well. Not all will go home until every last Redcoat is off this land."

"Okay, Thomas. I'm with you. Let's go and tell the general that we want to stay with him and help fight in any skirmishes he is called into until this war is completely over for the whole country."

So saying, the lads rode their horses over to their commander and informed him of their decision to stay with him. General Marion, not a man to show emotion readily, accepted their decision with a slight smile. "I'm glad to hear it, men," he said.

"I want to keep as many of the brigade with me as possible, but I know many have duties at their own homes to take care of, so I am happy to have you continue on as you have been doing. You have both been loyal and completed your duties well during your time as part of the brigade. I am about ready to leave for my headquarters at a nearby plantation as soon as everyone has decided what to do—go home or stay with me."

Will and Thomas looked around at all of the men as they got their personal belongings together to leave this theater of the war for a short time. Many would return if Marion needed them, but many would stay at home since the immediate danger to South Carolina seemed to have waned. Since both young men had their things with them already, they let their horses graze until the General and the rest of the militia were ready to leave.

In short order, after wishing his men an affectionate farewell, Marion and those who chose to remain with him left for an abandoned Tory plantation where Marion would set up his new headquarters. There he would await any orders from General Greene.

It didn't take long before he was back in his fighting clothes as he was summoned to take action against a mob of five hundred Tories. In the midst of the fighting a few hours later, were Thomas and Will, who barely fired any shots at the unruly mob. It only took a few blustering shots from the brigade to force the Tories to surrender.

"What are we going to do with all these Tories," wondered Will out loud.

"There are too many of them for us to imprison. We are only a few!"

"Let's wait and see what the general does," responded Will. "He knows our numbers. How few we are against them." So, they sat and waited for the decision of the Swamp Fox, who had outfoxed the enemy yet again! They watched as Marion rode his horse to the front of the line of Tories, who had already given up their weapons.

Speaking in a voice which allowed for no interference, he addressed the prisoners. "Men, I am giving you two choices. One, you can have your freedom on the condition that you take the oath to support the government and Patriot cause in South Carolina, or two, go to prison for the remainder of the war, at which time you will forfeit all of your wealth and properties to the Patriot cause."

"It's your decision. Talk among yourselves and let me know. I will give you fifteen minutes to come up with an answer." Marion then turned his horse away from the prisoners to give them time to discuss their choices.

"Wow!" Thomas said. "Not what I expected to hear him say."

"Me either," said Will. "However, knowing how much General Marion dislikes bloodshed, I am not surprised. They have to know by now that their cause is lost! Why hold a grudge? Why not give them a chance to become good Americans? I applaud our commander for his generous thinking."

They turned back to Marion, who once more rode to the forefront of the Tories. "So, men, what is your decision? Freedom or prison?"

To a man, all the Tories accepted the choice of freedom. They all lined up to pledge the oath to support the government of South Carolina. After the pledge was given, and they knew that if they broke that pledge, they would be hunted down and hung, all of the Tories headed back to their own homes, minus their weapons and ammunition.

As Thomas and Will watched the last Tory walk away from the brigade, Simon came barreling in toward the general. "Rider coming, Sir! From the looks of his uniform, it appears that he is a part of Washington's Continentals. Shall I bring him forward, Sir?"

"Yes, Simon. I don't know what General Washington wants with me now. Every time I turn around, there is something else to take care of, and between you and me, I'm getting tired. What say you, Simon? Are you ready for this war to end and go home to peace and quiet?"

"Yes, Sir, General Marion! I'm with you there. I'll go and get that man. He looks to be a colonel, Sir. It must be important for a colonel to be dispatched to deliver a message!"

Marion waved him off to do his bidding and sighed, wondering what the next mission was going to be. Waiting expectantly on the back of Bull, he watched as a young man, possibly in his late twenties, trotted toward him. The man lifted his hand in salute to the general, showing military respect for those higher in rank than they were.

"Whom do I have the honor of meeting, Colonel, as I see that is your rank in the Continental Army?" Marion asked as he answered the man's salute with one of his own.

"My name is Colonel Benjamin Sinclair, General Marion, given leave from General Washington to carry out a personal errand. I have been requested to find a young man, by the name of Thomas, who was last heard of as being a part of your militia. His parents had received a letter from General Greene way back in November of 1780, and this is now 1782. General Greene had indicated that he had been sent as a courier to deliver a message to you."

"Well, they were truly worried, and as I am an aide to General Washington, he gave me leave to find him. Would you have any idea where he might be, General Marion?"

Before Marion could answer, there was a loud whoop from further back behind the men. Thomas and Will had been observing the conversation between the general and this stranger and wondered what kind of message he had brought to the Swamp Fox. As Thomas had looked the stranger over, he saw some characteristics that belonged to only one person he knew, his brother, Ben.

All of a sudden, Colonel Sinclair heard, "Ben! Ben!"

"Well, General, I guess I have found the lost one! By your leave, Sir! May I greet my little brother?" General Marion smiled and shooed him away.

"Ben! Ben!" He heard again as a body all but knocked him off his feet.

"That's Colonel Ben to you, little brother," he said laughingly. Giving Thomas a big bear hug, he pushed himself back and looked at him up close. "You've grown an inch or two by the looks of it," he said.

"Mother and Father were beyond anxious when they heard that you were in the South fighting along with the Swamp Fox. Why didn't you send them a letter explaining where you were and why? I am here to take you home. You are desperately needed on the farm, and the war in this part of the country is all but finished. We've chased down the Redcoats and they have almost given up the rest of the country as well. We hope that they will be willing to see that their empire over here has collapsed."

"Now, let me go and give my proper respects and messages to General Marion before I am court-martialed!" He said with a smile. "I'll talk to you later."

"Okay," Thomas said, "but I want you to meet all my friends, especially Will who has been with me on a lot of adventures." Benjamin winked and nodded as he walked back toward the general, who had joyously watched their reunion.

"So sorry about that, Sir! I haven't seen my little brother since the war started. We were all worried about him. Thank you for taking such good care of him. It was hard to keep him penned down at home. He wanted to fight so much!"

"No trouble at all, Colonel," said Marion. "Do you have any information as to how the war is going farther North? Even as generals, we receive only scanty messages at best, and they are usually days and sometimes weeks old."

"Well, Sir. I can only tell you what I know. With the surrender of the British at Yorktown, General Washington said that the British at Charleston was the only active enemy group in South Carolina, as everyone in the North was already celebrating the end of the war. The British are evacuating that place as I speak. It appears, Sir, that the war will be really over once those soldiers in Charleston get on their ships."

"I understand that General Greene has them pretty well hemmed in, and as a result, the British and Tories have already burned supplies and rolled their cannons into the ocean so that we cannot use those guns against them."

Marion smiled. "I am sure that even as we speak, General Greene is already taking formal possession of the city and declaring that the war in South Carolina is over. This information relieves me no end. My men are weary, and even though they would continue the battle, if necessary, they are ready to get back to their own lives and families. I think that our fighting here is at an end, and I am joyous over our victory. We are no longer British subjects and now can begin to act as an independent nation. The whole country has earned it!"

"General Washington wanted to convey his utmost appreciation for you and your militia's actions during this war for our independence. You and your men have saved this part of the country by your bravery, skills, shrewdness, and brilliant strategies. He hopes that he will meet you in the near future as we set up a new government for the United States of America."

"I will be honored to meet him," said Marion. "We have all been fighting toward the same end. Now, about Thomas and Will, I will miss those two young men. They have been very important to me as couriers, spies, soldiers, guards, and whatever I needed them to be. They have always been willing to assist in the cause and have never disappointed me in their steadfastness. Their fathers can be very proud of those two boys. They have had many adventures which I am sure you will hear about in the near future. Just let me have a few words with them before you talk to them."

"Yes, General," responded Colonel Sinclair.

The two boys looked up as General Marion approached them. "Well, men," he said. "Your brother brings good news, Thomas. The war in the North has been finished for a while, and the only holdout, now, is Charleston. But it seems that General Greene has that already in hand, so it looks like our work here, as warriors, is done. You have both amazed me with your willingness to help fight this war. You have served as well as any seasoned man in my militia, and I am so proud of you both."

"Sir, it has been our privilege to serve under your leadership," interrupted Thomas. "We would gladly stay and help you in any way we can if you desire it."

"Thank you, Thomas. I appreciate those words but it seems that we are now able to go back to our previous lives. I will go back to my own plantation, repair it, and knowing myself very well, will probably become involved in building a new government in this new country. Even so, it is hard for me to say goodbye to those I have come to love and respect, and you two are part of that. Thomas, your brother has come to escort you back home, which I gladly give permission to him to do."

"Will, I know that your father is waiting impatiently for his heir to return to Francis Plantation and take over the reins there. If you continue as you have for me, he will be quite pleased with all your efforts."

As the general continued talking, the two boys looked at each other, knowing that their time together as very close friends would soon be coming to an end, and they were both saddened by this realization.

Marion looked at the two young men who had become almost like sons to him and felt a sadness that he had not anticipated. Swallowing the lump in his throat, he spoke again. "Men, I wish you Godspeed as you journey back to your homes. Remember that my plantation will always be open to you, and I wouldn't mind seeing you both again in the near future." With a salute to the boys, he wandered back to speak with Ben.

Striding up to the colonel, he said, "Please give my best regards to your parents for allowing their son, Thomas, to become a part of my militia. He has outdone himself, and I will truly miss him. He has my permission to leave with you as soon as you and he are ready. I am sure that he and Will want to say their goodbyes, too."

Saluting the General, Ben strode over to talk to Thomas and Will. He said, "Thomas, General Marion has given permission for you to leave and return home with me. How about it? Are you ready to go home? You have been away for almost two years and our parents are anxious to see you."

Thomas replied, "I am very happy to be returning home but I have made so many good friends here that I hesitate to leave them, especially Will, here, with whom I have had so many exciting adventures." Stepping over to his friend, Thomas put his arms over Will's shoulders and said, "I am really going to miss you, Will. Maybe, we can meet again soon. I would love to spend some time on your parents' plantation, and it would be fun to have you come and meet my family on our farm in New Hampshire."

"I would love that!" Will said. "I know that my father would gladly have you visit with us. You could meet my mother and all of my sisters. They would be sure to enjoy looking at a handsome face," he chuckled.

Thomas's face turned red at that comment, while Ben gave a loud belly laugh. "That would be fun," he ventured. "I have told you where I live and I already know your plantation's whereabouts, so why don't we plan to meet sometime in the next few months, after all the hubbub of this war has finally finished?"

"That would be great," replied Will. "I will expect to hear from you soon. Be careful on your way back home. There are still some angry Tories around that don't want to give up!"

"As General Marion often stated, watch your back, Will, until you are safely home." "With one last handshake, the boys went their separate ways, Will to head on back to the Francis Plantation and Thomas to make his way back to New Hampshire."

So ended the boys' time together with the Swamp Fox. Each one with memories that would last a lifetime.

Chapter 34

One year later

Astride Ebony, as in the past, Thomas rode through the gates of the Francis Plantation in South Carolina. He was relieved to see that there were no longer British troops stationed at the entrance or around the property. He was excited to meet up with Will again and finally meet those sisters of his. As he approached the front of the mansion, Will, dressed like a plantation owner, stepped down from the steps and quickly shook Thomas's hand as he alighted from his horse.

"I didn't think this day would ever come," said his friend. "I have missed those adventures that we had, but glad to be out of harm's way. Come and meet the rest of my family. You are looking much older, Thomas. When we first met, you were but fifteen, but after almost two years together, and birthdays missed, you are now closer to eighteen and I am almost twenty. How time flies! After we pay our respects to the family, let's sit down and catch up on what has gone on in the past year."

Hurrying up the steps and into the foyer, Will led Thomas into the parlor where his family was seated. First, he shook hands with Mr. Francis and asked about his health. Then he bowed to Mrs. Francis. Turning to face Will's sisters who were staring at him, his face suddenly went all red and he blustered about what to say. They were beauties, indeed, especially the one with the big blue eyes and blonde ringlets cascading down her back.

Will stepped in then, with a wide grin, and said, "Let me introduce my sisters, Thomas. The dark-haired beauty is Charlotte, but we call her 'Charlie'. She is sixteen. My next sister, the blue-eyed blonde, is Samantha, but she goes by 'Sammy'. She is your age, Thomas, almost eighteen," he said with laughter in his eyes. Both girls blushed as Will spoke about each of them. They obviously liked the look of Thomas, who had shown up in clothing befitting the son of a large landowner and horseman.

While they were eyeing each other, Will grabbed Thomas by the arm and exited the room with him. "Let's go to a quiet place and talk," he said. He led Thomas into the garden where they had talked with Will's father so long ago it seemed. But was it only about a year and a half ago that they had convinced Mr. Francis to assist them against the British? As they seated themselves on a bench, Will asked, "What have you been doing this past year, Thomas?"

"Well, when Ben and I arrived home, my parents gave a big birthday bash for me since I had missed two birthdays with them. They invited all of our neighbors to join us. Of course, they were enthralled with all of my stories. I have to admit, I was a little lavish in describing some of them, especially the one where we were abducted by a gang of thieves. I really poured it on, and some of the young ladies ended up swooning," Thomas laughed.

"Other than that, I have been working daily with my father and Ben, who has recently resigned his commission to come back and help father with the farm. Things are going well and father's horses are gaining a reputation for being some of the best in the Northeast. A lot of thanks goes to General Greene who recommended my father's horses to many of his friends."

"I was glad to hear from you, Thomas. Thanks for coming for this visit. I have been anticipating it for quite a while, as well as my sisters. I think they are both besotted with you." Again, Thomas's face turned red.

"Both of your sisters are very pretty, Will, but I have my eyes on another beauty at home. Her name is Barbara Ann, and I hope to wed her one day. What about you? Any young ladies in your life?"

"I was looking forward to having you as my brother-in-law, Thomas," Will said sadly. "But I understand. I, too, have set my sights on a young lady named Sharron, who lives two plantations over. She's eighteen and her father has given me permission to call upon her when the time comes. I hope to make her my wife by next spring. Father is retiring, so the plantation will come to me soon. There is a smaller home on the plantation that Father and Mother and my sisters will retire to when I marry and take over the running of the estate."

"However, I doubt that my sisters will remain unmarried for long. Many young men have been wooing them already."

"That is great news, Will! I am so happy for you," Thomas gushed. "So when will you come North to visit my home? Ben is next in line to take over the horse ranch but I have plans to build a home on some of the land that my father is giving me. I expect to start my own ranch eventually. In the meantime, I will keep assisting Ben and Father on the homestead. It would be wonderful if you could spend some of your honeymoon time in New Hampshire at our farm. There is plenty of room and you would love my parents."

"That's something I will have to discuss with the bride-to-be," laughed Will. "But it sounds like a plan to me. In the meantime, let me show you around the plantation before the dinner bell and let you get a better look than the last time you were here." Saying so, the young men rode around the estate discussing things that they were planning on for their futures. Through a revolutionary war, their friendship had been thoroughly cemented. Now, they both looked forward to a future that included sharing time in each other's homes and fulfilling their future hopes and dreams.

Unknowingly, down the road in a few short years, their lives would become entangled again, as a new war with Britain loomed on the horizon; they would all wonder if Britain would be the victor this time!

The End

Bibliography

Bass, R. D. (1978) *Ninety Six: The Struggle for the South Carolina Back Country*, Lexington, SC: The Sandlapper Store, Inc.

Bass, R. D. (1974) *Swamp Fox: The Life and Campaigns of General Francis Marion*, Orangeburg, SC: Sandlapper Publishing Co., Inc.

Brown, R. W. Jr. (2009) *King's Mountain and Cowpens: Our Victory was Complete*, Charleston, SC: The History Press.

Campbell, C. (2021) *General Francis Marion, Irregular Life of an Irregular Warrior*, Coppell, TX: Craig Campbell.

Holbrook, S. H. (2008) *The Swamp Fox of the Revolution*, New York: Sterling.

James, W. D. (2013) *Swamp Fox: General Francis Marion and His Guerrilla Fighters of the American Revolutionary War*, U.S.A.: William Dobein James.

O'Donnell, P. K. (2016) *Washington's Immortals: The Untold Story of an Elite Regiment Who Changed the Course of the Revolution*, New York.

Oller, J. (2016) *The Swamp Fox: How Francis Marion Saved the American Revolution*, Boston, MA: Da Capo Press.

O'Reilly, B., Dugard, M. (2017) *Killing England: The Brutal Struggle for American Independence*, NY: Henry Holt and Company.

Weems, P. M. L., Horry, Brig. Gen. P. (2004) *The Life of General Francis Marion: A Celebrated Partisan Officer, in the Revolutionary War, Against the British and Tories in South Carolina and Georgia*, Winston-Salem, NC: John F. Blair Publisher.

Wikipedia: Cowpens.

http://www.Patriotresource.com.

http://www.doublgv.com/ggv/battles/tactics.ktml

www.FrancisMarionTrail.com-clarendon county, SC

http://www.battlefields.org >revolutionary-war >battles